———————

Mondrala Press wishes to thank all its friends, fans, patrons, and investors for making this book possible, and especially:

Ms. Randa Dumanian
Mr. and Mrs. Karol and Dagmara Maziukiewicz
de domo Sowul

without whose enthusiasm and open hearts this book could never have happened.

———————

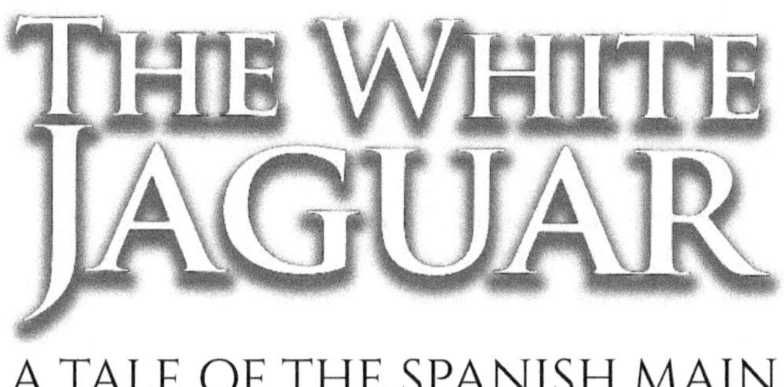

THE WHITE JAGUAR

A TALE OF THE SPANISH MAIN

VOLUME 3
LASANA

BY ARKADY FIEDLER
TRANSLATED BY TOM PINCH

MONDRALA
PRESS

Mondrala Press is an imprint of
Ringel & Esch, S.A.R.L.-S
www.mondrala.com

ISBN epub and kindle: 978-2-919820-57-3
ISBN Paperback: 978-2-919820-58-0
ISBN Hardcover: 978-2-919820-59-7

Edited by Mondrala Press
Cover Design by Mondrala Press

The cover uses elements of an adobe stock image 581168482 by Demencial Studies,
"Beautiful Woman of the Amazon, Power and Beauty of the Indigenous Culture of
the Amazon."

ABOUT THE AUTHOR

Arkady Fiedler (1894—1985) was a Polish writer, journalist and adventurer. He studied philosophy and natural science in Kraków, Poznań and Leipzig. He took part in the Greater Poland Uprising in 1918 and was one of the founders of the Polish Military Organization. He travelled extensively and wrote 32 books which have been translated into 23 languages and sold over 10 million copies in total. His most famous book, Squadron 303 about the legendary Polish fighter squadron in the Battle of Britain, sold over 1.5 million copies and was recently published in English
by Aquila Polonica Publishing.

ABOUT THIS BOOK

This is the first episode in a 5 volume series entitled *The White Jaguar*, a fictionalized account of the life and adventures of John Bober, a Virginian renegade and an Arawak chief in Guyana in the first half of the 18th century.

ABOUT MONDRALA PRESS

Mondrala Press publishes English translations of
great Polish books—books with a track record of international
critical and commercial success but which, for political reasons, have
never been published in English. And now, finally, they are.
Be the first to discover this new territory!

To see our newest titles or to subscribe to our newsletter,
please visit

WWW.MONDRALA.COM
THE GREATEST BOOKS YOU HAVE NEVER HEARD OF

TRANSLATOR'S SPECIAL REQUEST

Translating and publishing this book has been a labor of love for me.
I grew up reading it, and I have always wanted to be able
to share it with my American friends. And so here it is.
It will not make me rich, but if you liked the book, would you please
recommend it to a friend?
And give it an Amazon review?
https://www.amazon.com/dp/2919820494

THANK YOU!

THE WHITE JAGUAR

Angostura to Essequibo, 1727

TABLE OF CONTENTS

The Covenant with the Warao

The upriver voyage was easy: at high tide, the swift current carried us inland, and the schooner, catching the gusty winds from the ocean in its sails, helped us make good progress. When the tide changed after several hours, and we found ourselves battling the current, we dropped anchor near the shore and waited for the next tide.

By God! How fantastically—how insanely!—frothed and boiled all around us the richness of nature! I have heard many a tall tale, and yet how could I not fall into raptures looking at the world around me? How many sorts of strange, gigantic fish splashed about us in the muddy currents, jumping out above the surface of the water! How many monkeys showed up in the branches of the coastal trees! What mysterious croakings, whistlings, and gurglings stirred our imagination! And what a stunning sight it was—for the eye and for the heart—when high overhead flew in the sky the most beautiful of birds in the world, huge parrots, radiating an incredible whimsy of colored feathers—miraculous birds, called *arakanga* and *ararauna* by the Indians.

And the forest, the forest that covered both river shores! The forest was mad, insane, fairy tale, enchanted, lush, intensely green, pulsating with the noise of a billion insects, wildly confused, battling against itself, intertwined. A wilderness completely impenetrable without a machete—a wilderness beyond human comprehension and humming with a billion insects! I, born and bred in the Virginia forest, fed on the forest, its child and devoted lover—I would think myself in paradise—if not for these blasted insects! Their swarms, especially the monstrous, evil-stinging mosquitoes and midges from hell, day and night poisoned our life. And now I understood that the Spanish shirts and trousers would have to be apologized to and donned again, especially when crossing the undergrowth. The feet also needed protection, so I had the women make me sandals from the horsehide we had on board.

Arasibo's handicap lay in his left leg, once broken and then badly fused, shorter than the right. The heavy Spanish boots proved not worth spit. Thinking about the problem, I came up with the idea that the lame man should wear sandals like me; only the left one should have a much thicker sole. The idea was simple, but its consequences revolutionary: Arasibo lost his limp. The invalid was constitutionally unable to express a human sentiment, but I noticed that he was profoundly affected and ready to jump hoops in thanks.

Two war dugouts followed in our wake—besides the one gifted to me by Jekuana—a second one worked its way up the Orinoco, paddled by twenty Warao, all armed up to their teeth. Jekuana himself sailed with us on the schooner while several of my Arawak friends transferred to our war canoe and paddled along. The easy fellowship established in the village continued. There was no end to cheerful songs, and people were eager to chat with each other.

We were still a whole day away from Kaiiwa when the Orinoco, wide like a bay at its mouth, finally gained the appearance of a river, a few miles wide, yes, but clearly a river.

We had not spotted any trace of human presence thus far, but now we heard the sound of drums wafting towards us from the forest. As we passed, the inhabitants of these shores, invisible in their jungle, seized their wooden drums and beat them like there was no tomorrow. We could hear them from very far away, and the music they made sounded both happy and astonishing at the same time. Jekuana glowed and said to me:

"They welcome you, White Jaguar! You are their brother!"

"Is it Warao over there?"

"Yes!"

Sometimes, a small boat peeled off from the shore, with two or three oarsmen waving their hands from a distance, giving us friendly signals.

Before we arrived at the village of Oronapi, I summoned Manauri, Arnak, and Vagura to caucus together.

"Have Arawaks and the Warao always been such great friends?" I asked them.

"No," replied Manauri matter-of-fact. "The Warao have often quarreled with us."

"So, how do you explain their current love for you?"

"Things have changed."

"Don't you find it strange?"

"No."

"I do!" interjected Arnak.

"I tell you, there is nothing mysterious about this," Manauri reassured us with the enigmatic smile of a man in on a secret. "And, at any rate, it is not about us, the Warao and the Arawaks, but about you, Yan!"

"That's the part I do not get."

"And I do. Do you recall how Jekuana said last night that war awaited us behind every bush? It seems to me it was not a joke. And you have the fame of a victorious commander."

"Because you keep telling everyone I am, you chatterbox!" I growled.

"I do, but not without cause. I must talk like this!"

"What's the war, Manauri? Against the Spaniards?"

"No."

"Who then?"

"I still don't know. But there is no shortage of Caribs around."

"And the Warao are not Caribs?"

"No."

The prospect of becoming involved in some unspecified Indian war was not to my liking, but I gathered from various signs that it suited Manauri fine. Did he reckon that amid the turmoil of war, he would find it easier to regain influence in his former tribe?

As we approached the abode of Oronapi, which the Warao called Kaiiwa, the drums onshore beat ever more zealously—all night without ceasing—and in places, their booming came from many directions at once. At such times, it seemed as if the whole jungle gave us a noisy, triumphant welcome.

As we approached Kaiiwa itself, I had to put on the Spanish captain's uniform again, the gold braids, the heavy boots, and the jaguar skin, and forget neither the silver pistol nor the mother-of-pearl sword nor—most importantly, according to Manauri's instructions— the defiant and threatening glare that went with them.

Unlike Jekuana's village, Kaiiwa did not have a central terrace. Its numerous huts stood here and there, a good distance apart, on stilts impaled in the ground. In the shade of the biggest of them, set back some two hundred paces from the shore, Oronapi awaited us at the head of his elders. Everyone, but most of all Oronapi, was dressed in colorful feathers, necklaces, and fresh body paint, and at their sides, they had richly carved maces. Only the commander-in-chief sat on a stool, but there were several empty seats beside him, evidently in keeping with the traditional ceremonial reserved for us.

As we landed, Oronapi did not come to greet us as Jekuana had but continued to sit in state, dignified, motionless, waiting for us to approach. I walked slowly towards him, surrounded by Manauri, Jekuana, Arnak, Vagura, and Fujudi. Oronapi remained seated.

He was a proud man and wanted to emphasize his superior position as chief and host and would not greet us until we approached closer.

After we traveled about half the distance, Manauri whispered to me to stop. I did. Then Jekuana, despite his obesity, swiftly sprang to my side and, full of animation and politeness, invited me to continue my march. But Manauri growled at him to keep his mouth shut and to go on without us. Jekuana fell silent, panting worriedly and not knowing what to do.

Oronapi, seeing what was afoot, gave up his posture of dignified indifference and stood up. He approached us with a tread less measured and dignified than was his due. Already from a distance, he showed joy and cried out eagerly:

"Come on, friends! Come on! Come boldly, come cheerfully, come assuredly!"

Repeating these words of ritual greeting, he approached me, took me by the hand, and, amid loud voices of welcome coming from his entourage, led me into the shade of his hut.

And now all formality was gone. Standing in front of Oronapi's stool, I studied it with a show of attention, as if fascinated, and finally asked with feigned seriousness:

"Is this stool really so comfortable that a man, once having sat down, finds it hard to get up from it again?"

Oronapi understood my thickly laid allusion, accepted it merrily, and immediately asked me to sit on the stool:

"Try it, White Jaguar, and see for yourself!"

So, with great ceremony, I sat down on the chief's stool.

And then the singing began, and the dancing, and the devouring of grilled fish, game, and sweet fruit, interspersed frequently with much drinking of *kashiri* (in which, taught by my earlier experience, I only dipped my mouth), in a word: the feast began in earnest, so enthusiastically and in such a cordial mood that it surpassed all our expectations.

At a certain point, I whispered to Arnak, in English, of course:

"Do you get this, Arnak? I sure don't!"

"This hospitality is extraordinary. It is true!"

"Are these people always so welcoming?"

"I never met them, but Manauri says no."

"A war, then?"

"Surely, a war."

He said it with such unshakable confidence that it made me burst out laughing. Not at him, but at the situation: what sort of a war was afoot if the people threatened by it were ready to feast and celebrate with such gusto?

Oronapi, unlike the jovial Jekuana, seemed to be of a rather sullen and stern disposition and had a somewhat brusque manner, but on this day, he went out of his way to be polite. He was positively oozing kindness and desire to please. He cared about us so much that his efforts made me chuckle, and finding myself in a pink mood on account of all the *kashiri* mouth-dipping, I asked him—perhaps too brusquely—to what favorable winds I should attribute his extraordinary hospitality and politeness.

Oronapi looked at me, surprised by my question. But his confusion did not last long. He became serious. He stared thoughtfully at the *kashiri* gourd, which he held in his hand, and after a moment, poured the drink far away as a sign that he didn't want to drink anymore.

"I want to make an alliance with you!" he said finally with great emphasis, looking me hard in the eye. "I want your friendship, White Jaguar!"

"I have guessed as much," I replied light-heartedly, not wishing to fall into his solemn tone. "But why?"

"You want to know? I want to make an alliance with you because you know how to fight: you and your people."

"Is the matter so important?"

"Yes, it is so important!"

There was a moment of silence.

"Listen now, White Jaguar, and I will tell you."

And Oronapi made his request, addressed less to me than to Manauri, that we should go no farther and settle just outside his village, where a thick forest grew on the elevated shore and where there was plenty of fertile land for cultivation. Oronapi promised to give us all the help we needed clearing the land and building our village, and seeing as there were only a few women among us, he promised to assign the healthiest and strongest Warao girls as wives and companions to all single men on our ship.

Our Arawaks were very pleased to hear these words, for the

kashiri had warmed their minds, and the Warao girls bustling about were not unsightly at all.

But Manauri thanked Oronapi politely for his very generous offer and declared that he could not accept the invitation, for it was his duty to rejoin his tribe.

"But I will never forget your words," he concluded. "And I take White Jaguar for my witness that I will always remember your hospitality, your kind words, and I will always come to your aid, even if I must fight a war in your defense. I, in turn, assume that if we are ever in need, you will come to our aid."

"Yes, I will. We will," Oronapi hastened with his reassurance.

Irritated with all this polite diplomatic footwork, I asked the chief point blank to tell me openly what was coming, for I liked to know what I promised.

"You are right! I have not explained!" said Oronapi. "And you should know what threatens us here."

While the party went on in earnest—dancing, singing, and beating of drums—the several of us—Oronapi, Jekuana, Manauri, Fujudi, Arnak, Vagura, and I—sat closer together and listened attentively to what Oronapi told us and Fujudi translated.

To the west, on the shores of the Orinoco, were Spanish settlements. They were generally peaceful, but in the south, near the sea, on the rivers Essequibo, Demerara, Berbice, Cayena,[1] in a land called Guyana, lived the Dutch, the English, and the French. They had come as traders to trade their manufactured goods for Indian products, and as long as they were only trading, all was fine.

The Dutch were the most numerous, and they had been the first to set up plantations to grow various valuable cash crops. For this work, they needed the services of native peoples, but as the Indians were not numerous and not eager to toil, and the plantations multiplied like the voracious *sipari* fish, the Dutch began to look for other ways to secure labor.

---

[1] Cayenne River, which gave its name to Cayenne pepper and... Guyana

Various Indian nations lived in the south. There were Arawaks near the sea and their relatives, the Wapishana deeper in the forest, and Atorao, and Tarum, who were only a branch of the Wapishana. However, apart from these peaceful tribes, devoted mainly to agriculture, there were others: Caribs, greedy, aggressive, eager for war and plunder. The most dangerous among them were the Akawaio and the Karibis, both marauding close to the sea and, inland, the Macushi and the Arecuna—that is, the Taulipang. They ranged deep in the forest, all the way to the *llanos*.

The Dutch got along with the Indians variously, sometimes fraternizing, sometimes warring against them; yet, when they began to experience a shortage of hands on their plantations, some of the Caribs, the most warlike ones, smelled an opportunity and offered to supply captive slaves. Soon, their hordes, armed by the Dutch, made daring raids on neighboring tribes—the Akawaio slave-hunting in the west and north, where they came right up to the shores of the Orinoco and Karibis to the west and south, carrying the war and plunder as far as upper Essequibo and the Rupununi. As a result of the slave-raiding, some parts of the country turned into uninhabited wasteland.

Everywhere they went, they left a trail of tears and destruction as they dragged all whom they managed to capture alive to the Dutch plantations.

"And has this gone on for long?" I asked.

"For many, many years. But lately, it has been worse."

"And those attacked do not defend themselves? Just take it like baby does? Don't you have maces, spears, and bows?"

"We do. But they are more skilled at war, experienced in robbery, and quicker to spill blood. We farm and fish. It gives us no joy to cut other men's throats. And the Akawaio have better weapons: the Dutch give them matchlocks. Who can oppose that?"

"And have you fought back?"

"We have. But they are stronger than us. I am sorry to have to admit it. Some of us were killed, others were taken captive. Now, the only way open to us is to escape."

"Has it come to this? Is the enemy more numerous than you?"

Oronapi assured me that the Akawaio were indeed more numerous than the Warao, but both Jekuana and Fujudi corrected him: the Akawaio usually attacked in small groups of only a dozen warriors each, very rarely a couple of dozen. But no one could match their cunning, their ferocity, their agility, and their readiness to kill and torture. They were jaguars incarnate.

"And have they attacked our Arawaks on the Imataca?" Manauri asked.

"Openly—not yet," said Fujudi. "But last dry season, our hunters went hunting in the Imataca Mountains to the south and mysteriously disappeared. All trace of them was lost. And then we heard about an Akwaio slaving party prowling in that region."

"The dry season is upon us," took up Oronapi. "There is less rain every day now. The rivers are falling. This is a good time to make war. Word has reached us that the Akawaio of the Cuyuni[2] are readying against us."

"Maybe they are already on the way?"

"Maybe."

The solid wall of the jungle was no more than a hundred paces from the cottages. Apparently, the Kaiiwa people had their fields elsewhere, deeper in the forest. How easy it would be for the enemy to sneak up on them right now!

"Oronapi, have you set up sentries?"

"What?"

He did not understand why one would set up sentries in peacetime, and when he finally got my explanation of this totally otherworldly concept, he shrugged in surprise.

"No," he said simply.

"You must set up sentries! Day and night."

"You say?" he murmured unconvinced.

And the feast went on without any security measures.

---

[2] A left bank tributary of the Essequibo.

The story of the Akawaio reminded me of the warlike Haudenosaunee of North America. Perhaps the Akawaio could be called the Iroquois of the South.[3] With all this, I couldn't help but be amazed by the recklessness of our hosts. Their carelessness tempted fate and invited danger.

On that day, an alliance was established between Oronapi, Manauri, and me: we solemnly pledged to come to each other's defense and assistance. To seal the alliance, Oronapi gave us two boats, one large, burnt from a large tree trunk, called *itauba* after the tree from which it was made, the other one small, made out of bark, called *yabota*, so that (he said) we could swiftly come to his aid in need, whereupon I presented the chief with a Spanish sword, even more elaborately ornamented than the one which I had given to Jekuana.

Apart from this, we gave him one of our Spanish boats.

We spent the night in Kaiiwa, but for safety's sake, I had all my companions sleep on the schooner, and I posted sentries. The good ship has become our home, our faithful friend. It was our rock and our fortress.

I woke up in the middle of the night to check the sentries. Unfortunately, I found the men asleep. Likewise, the inhabitants of Kaiiwa were all fast asleep. Only a few small dogs barked here and there, and the forest made its usual nocturnal racket.

The following morning, as soon as the high tide came and the river began to swell, we set off on our journey, cordially bid farewell by our new allies, the Warao.

---

[3] Haudenosaunee, also known as the Five Nations (later the Six Nations) were a famously warlike confederacy of Iroquois-speaking Native Americans in the northeast North America and Upstate New York.

The Chief and his Sorcerer

When I was a child, my mother told me the story of the Greek hero Odysseus, who had wandered the seas for ten years before he returned to his homeland. And now my Arawak friends seemed to me just like him, returning to their families after years of captivity. They were overjoyed at the prospect of the approaching encounter. The thought that they would soon see their relatives and friends made them both ecstatic and focused at the same time.

On the second day after leaving Kaiiwa, we gathered on the deck of the schooner to talk and make plans. I myself did not speak. Manauri had the floor, and I could see that he was troubled by the uncertainty of the coming days. He found it easy to move our friends: those stormclouds, approaching in the south from the direction of the fierce Akawaio, threatened to invade the shores of the Orinoco, our shores, and the best proof of this was not just the warnings of the Warao, but chiefly their unusually friendly behavior.

What conclusions followed from this for us? To stay close together, as we have thus far. All of us on the ship should act like one family, bound by brotherly love—all the more so as we were crowned with the glory of victorious battles against the Spaniards and as the fame of our invincible arms preceded us.

Manauri's words went straight to our hearts, and we gladly accepted his summons to unite into a single clan, to which, of course, those on the Imataca were to be granted admission if they so wished.

But here, a significant question arose.

"If we are to become a single lineage, what should our totem be?"

"Why, the Spanish ship!"

"Foolishness!" Manauri winced. "Clans derive from animals and bear animal names!"

"There is only one name for us, then," said the lame Arasibo. "The Jaguar Clan."

"Impossible!" Manauri shook his head. "A Jaguar Clan already exists, and Coneso is its chief."

"I know," Arnak spoke up. "We will call ourselves the Clan of the White Jaguar!"

"That is an excellent idea!" Arasibo applauded him with zeal.

All the Indians now turned their questioning eyes at me, for the name of White Jaguar has somehow become my property. I was against it. Let them call the clan as they please, as long as it is of benefit to its members and to the whole tribe, but why associate it with me?

"Oh, but yes, it will be of benefit!" exclaimed Arasibo.

His elation imparted itself to others because, like Manauri, they did not know what awaited them at Imataca, while the unity of our group was palpable, sincere, and promised durability.

However, there was someone on the ship who frowned at all this—Fujudi. He had joined us on the sailing ship only a few days ago, and, of course, no one thought to invite him to the family. And now he gave a speech warning us in harsh tones, which sounded almost like a threat, that the formation of such a new lineage may undermine the old order which had held for generations and threaten the internal harmony of the whole tribe.

"You will only anger our elders!" he admonished us severely. "Coneso will not like it at all. And here you are choosing a name so close to that of his own clan!"

"The name is a good name!" boomed Arasibo.

Fujudi looked at him sharply, held him in his gaze for a long time, then said scathingly:

"You, son of a cayman, better keep your trap shut! Don't imagine that your foul deeds have been forgotten!"

These words had an unexpected effect as if they had lashed the invalid with a whip. For an instant, something like fear flickered in his eyes. He immediately cooled down and seemed to shrink.

"What misdeeds?" asked Manauri.

But Fujudi waved his hand dismissively.

"What's the point of talking? Better not mention it!"

"Since you started it, you better finish," insisted Manauri with steel in his voice.

"He is a hooligan, a brawler, a vandal," said Fujidi, pointing a damning finger at Arasibo.

"Explain it!"

The guilt of Arasibo was heavy: he had committed a sacrilege. While still living with the rest of the Arawaks at Mount Vulture, he refused to submit to a decision made by the sorcerer Carapana against his family. He dared to oppose the command, to undermine the wizard's authority. Why, the mad slanderer did not shrink from insult, proclaiming that Carapana was a weak sorcerer. It was only thanks to his accident with his leg and his disability that Arasibo was not put to death and merely abandoned at Mount Vulture.

All present now turned to the invalid with horror and astonishment—that such a sluggish fellow had been capable of such impudence.

"Was this so?" the chief asked him sternly.

"It was," murmured Arasibo, but the defiance in his her eyes made it clear that he didn't feel guilty.

"Maybe the sorcerer had acted unjustly?" I stood up for the invalid.

No one answered me. I wasn't even sure that anyone paid attention. Apparently, the dignity of a sorcerer was untouchable, his judgments beyond questioning.

"I do not know why the creation of a new lineage should anger tribal elders," said Manauri provocatively, referring to Fujudi's speech.

"Coneso will not like it," replied Fujidi curtly.

"He will not like it?"

"He will not allow it."

The chief impatiently bit his lips. His eyes grew dark like a storm cloud.

"But he will have to allow us to rejoin the tribe!"

"He will undoubtedly allow that."

"And he will know that we have lived in captivity for many

years."

"He knows this already."

"And that we have seen many things in the world, learned many new things, and that our cruel fate has taught us wisdom. He has to understand that we have become tougher and smarter and more resilient and less fearful."

Manauri laid things out clearly for all to see: he obviously had a mind of his own. His companions listened to him with wrapt attention while all Fujudi had as his argument was a fussy face. After a moment of silence, Fujudi asked:

"And who will be the head of your clan?"

Manauri and several Arawaks looked at me.

"No!" I objected. "Not me! I will leave you soon and sail south, down to the English factories. Manauri is your head and your leader!"

The jungle on both shores of the river stood on monstrous swamps impassable to the human foot. For miles and miles, trees sprouted straight out of the water or from a waterlogged morass. There was hardly a clump of dry earth anywhere. The odor of rotting vegetation, which wafted towards us from the swamp, was in places so intoxicating that it made us feel nauseous. No one could possibly survive here, you would think. And yet, how luxuriant, how blazing an animal life boiled in this inhuman wilderness. The jungle positively teemed with birds, and billions upon billions of insects hummed in the steamy air.

It was then that I saw the most amazing butterflies of my life: so gigantic that, in deep shock, I at first refused to believe my eyes.

They were as big as two hands and as bright blue as the sky, but in the sun, they gleamed like metal. They flew out of the forest and circled above our ship. There was something captivating about them: with their azure, they transported one to some happy fairy-tale land— they were so strange and so spell-binding—making one feel he was dreaming. My Indian friends added to their magic, saying that they were ghosts of the forest—*hebu*—and sometimes could be malicious. I could not reconcile in my mind malice and their extraordinary beauty and laughed off my friend's tall tales.

The strangeness and vastness of nature that surrounded us overwhelmed the soul. This wilderness seemed so mighty in its ominous majesty that human affairs and concerns were overshadowed by it and seemed to become but a negligible trifle and sometimes disappeared from sight altogether, as the light of a candle disappears in direct sunlight.

One day, of an afternoon, we saw in the south the faint outlines of vast, low-lying hills covered with dense forests. These were the tail end of a great mountain range that Pedro called Sierra Imataca. The range, he said, stretched nearly 500 miles from west to southeast and formed a barrier behind which the famed Cuyuni River rolled its waters to the Essequibo. The sight of the distant hills alone was a relief: at least there was a break in the endless marshes.

The home of the Arawaks on the Imataca lay several miles from the place where the tributary entered the Orinoco, but even before we approached its mouth, the shores, though still swampy, seemed to imbue with grace and good news.

The news of our approach had run ahead of us, and now people rowed out to see us. From the coastal reeds and floodplains, their boats splashed towards our ship. It was the Arawak natives welcoming their returning countrymen, fathers looking for their sons, brothers for their brothers, many coming on the deck of our sailing ship and filling it with cheerful chatter.

Only me they approached with great timidity. They barely dared look me in the face, full of fear and worshipful awe as if I were an unearthly being. Only when they saw that I was a common man like everyone else and friendly to them did they become bolder.

"They say that you are bringing a great treasure," Manauri explained to me with a chuckle.

He beamed. He had not been forgotten during all the years of his absence. People remembered him, recognized him, welcomed him with warmth and respect. It only hurt him a little that among those who had come to greet him, there was no sign of Pirokai, his brother, the present head of the family, a man, as Manauri had often told me, unkind and envious. Anyway, none of the elders came to see us on the ship: we were greeted only by the common people and the ordinary warriors. But they greeted us warmly and with unexpected joy.

On the fourth day after leaving Kaiiwa, we approached the seat of the head chief of this branch of the Arawaks, Coneso. The settlement was called Serima, and it lay on a dry bank of the Imataca, surrounded by a magnificent high-canopy forest. We had left behind the swamps of the Orinoco.

The last day of our great journey was hot and stuffy, there was no wind and no sun, the world lay covered in a thin veil of white haze. My Indians told me again to assume the captain's gala outfit. They themselves also got dressed up: they put on various Spanish shirts and robes, and at their sides, they hung captured cutlasses and foils. They looked deliciously quirky.

I was struck by Lasana's excitement. Clearly, she wanted to pull me aside to talk, but somehow, in the last hours of bustle and preparations for landing, this proved impossible. Yet, she had business with me—I could see it from her frequent glances.

"What's with her?" I asked Arnak.

"No clue. Some girly mood," the boy shrugged his shoulders.

"She seems uneasy. What's gotten to her?"

Arnak was lost for an answer, but at one point, when we were near, I summoned her to me.

"What ails the Charming Palm?" I asked her point blank. "What do you need?"

"I don't need anything."

The woman became abashed, which made her look still prettier than usual. She tried to veil her large eyes under her long lashes.

"Are you afraid of something?"

"Yes, I'm afraid of something," she admitted honestly.

"Everyone is overjoyed, but you are afraid? That's backwards!" I pretended to scold her.

"And Manauri?" she reminded me with a perverse twitch in the corners of her mouth. "Is he also happy and calm?"

"Heh, what a comparison! He's the chief. He has things to worry about, but you—you are a young woman."

"You see, exactly, I am a young woman!" she said clearly annoyed.

"And very good-looking!" I praised her with a smile, hoping to put her in a better mood.

But this time, she did not take up the banter. Her heart was heavy.

"Tell me, will you? What are you afraid of?" I asked.

"The land!" she replied. "Our tribe. It's laws. Separations."

This sounded both mysterious and ominous. But there was no time to explain the intricacies of Indian customs. And maybe Lasana balked at saying too much in front of Arnak, our mediator?

"Yan!" she said suddenly, firmly, looking me directly in the face with a serious expression. "Do you remember how you defended our comrades, the Africans when the Spaniards wanted to take them into captivity?"

"On the *llanos*? Yes, I remember."

"Yes. You said then that the Africans were under your protection and that the Spaniards did not dare touch them. Take me now under your protection!"

"You, Lasana?"

"Yes, me. A woman. Protect me like a man of my family."

She said it with such simplicity and gentleness that I wanted to laugh. Ha! She had tricked me, little minx! There was no way I could refuse her request.

"Very well. I take you under my protection, Charming Palm!"

The Imataca was not a wide river but very deep and still subject to the tides of the distant ocean. It allowed us to tie the ship only a few paces from the shore. Our hosts threw several tree trunks from the shore to the ship, and we were able to descend without entering the water and even lead down our last remaining horse.

Like all the Indian villages I have seen, Serima was not a densely built-up village. Her huts lay scattered about a good distance from each other. We had landed in the middle of the settlement.

Coneso, richly dressed in a headdress and various strings of forest beads, awaited us, surrounded by elders in the shade of a large *toldo*—a roofed structure without walls. At first, the ceremonial of welcome appeared to unfold like our visits with Oronapi and Jekuana, but as we passed the midpoint between the river and the chief's entourage, a significant thing caught my attention: next to Coneso, who sat on the chief's stool, there sat another man, an old man, while the rest of the elders, as usual, remained standing. What particularly worried me, however, was the lack of free stools for us, the arrivals. Did Coneso want us to stand while he remained sitting?

"Arnak, do you see?" I whispered. "There are no stools."

"I see."

"What to do?"

"Maybe stop and wait? Let Coneso will come to us?"

"No, he will not come... we will do something else! We have our own stools on the ship. Vagura! Hop on board and fetch two! And fast!"

Vagura understood in an instant and ran back to the ship.

"Who Is this old man next to Coneso?" I asked Manauri when we resumed our slow progress towards the chief.

"Carapana, the sorcerer."

"Is he so important that he may sit?"

"He's the brain and the right hand of the chief. Nothing happens in our tribe without his say-so."

According to Indian tradition, the host usually waited for the guests to approach while seated on his stool, but when they did, he rose

Adam and Eve as Amerian Indians
Source Unknown, Wellcome Collection

to greet them. Not Coneso. Coneso remained firmly seated on his stool. He watched us and remained stubbornly silent. And no stoolshad been prepared for us.

The reluctance and rudeness of the chief and his retinue made an unpleasant impression but also made me chuckle because they were so very different from the effusive cordiality with which the rest of the tribe had welcomed us.

Just at that moment, Vagura came running. He brought a single stool—in his hurry, he had no time to find more, he explained in a whisper. Without thinking, I offered the stool he had brought to Manauri, and with a sweeping motion, I took off my jaguar skin and my captain's frock coat and told Arnak to fold them up so that they formed a pile, on which I sat with exaggerated contentment as if it was my customary way to sit.

The Arawak elders watched all this activity with great curiosity tinged with not a little fear. They must have sensed some symbolic rite, just as once the Warao did at Jekuana's. They were clearly uneasy about the magical powers I or my clothing might possess.

Is there a greater power than the power of the jaguar itself? The prudent Manauri knew well what he was doing when he demanded that I wear the skin at every ceremonial opportunity.

Coneso, a man of great age and stature, seemed to me taller and more muscular than other Arawaks. His face was conceited and puffed up, but what was most striking—almost painful—was the mark of greedy voluptuousness. The plump mouth expressed a perverted sensuality, the eyes gleamed lustfully. And yet, even at that moment, neither defiant pride nor sensual desires could hide the uncertainty that the commander-in-chief felt in the depths of his soul.

Unlike Carapana, the sorcerer. He was very, very old; deep wrinkles lined his face, but his eyes were keen and young. He was sitting erect, rigid, without the slightest movement, his hands resting on his knees. You'd think he was a sculpted forest idol—only his gaze seemed to devour us, staring at us as if he wanted to pierce us with his eyes. He was very composed, sullen, and inscrutable. I sensed in him a cold-blooded man, capable of every cruelty and every betrayal and ready to kill anyone who would dare oppose his will. Not in vain did the Arawaks fear him like the plague.

To the other side of Coneso stood a small, slender man with lively, narrow eyes. He almost disappeared under the splendor of ornaments made of colorful belts and bird feathers, as if the rich outfit had been designed to hide the insignificance of the person. This was Pirokai, the brother of Manauri, that dangerous schemer. He looked at his brother now, but I did not read much joy in his gaze.

We sat for a while without saying a word, staring at each other. At last, Coneso grunted, and he opened his mouth. But instead of a flowery greeting, to which the Warao accustomed me, I heard a hoarse and rather indifferent murmur, directed half at Manauri and half at me:

"Are you... tired?"

Was that the first thing to say? Bloody murder!

"No," grunted Manauri.

"Are you hungry?" asked Coneso next.

"No," repeated my companion.

As the chief was not very talkative, we, too, were not generous with words.

"I am hungry," I said. "All of us are hungry."

Barely had Arnak translated my words, but Coneso ordered women standing nearby to bring food and drink.

"You misunderstood me, chief!" I said. "I did not have food in mind."

"What then?"

"We were hungry for warm words of welcome."

Coneso was unimpressed:

"Did my people not offer you warm words?" he asked, confrontation in his voice. "Didn't they come to you on the river and welcome you like brothers?"

"They—yes, they did. But you? You do not."

"I have plenty of time for that," the chief cut me off with a sour expression. He turned towards the women, bringing baskets full of food and large jugs with the indispensable *kashiri,* and he supervised the serving to make sure that everyone got equal measure: us, the thirty guests, and his retinue of elders.

With clear displeasure, he raised his cup to me and Manauri, and gave a signal to start the revelries. But how different they were from those among the Warao: how muffled, how forced, how devoid of shouts of joy, how free of smiles!

The sorcerer Carapana said nothing did not eat or drink. He just sat there imperturbable and smoked tobacco from a long bamboo pipe. Letting out a cloud of smoke from time to time, he looked at us with a cold, impassive, but persistent gaze as if he was impressing an invisible seal on our faces.

I sensed that our lame Arasibo feared his gaze. He crouched down behind my back, but even there, the eyes of the sorcerer found him.

At the behest of Coneso, Manauri told the story of his people's captivity on Margarita Island, their escape from there, and all that followed. His tale took a long time. The people of the village, having surrounded us in a dense circle, listened with bated breath, and even the elders softened a little, relaxing their cold restraint.

When Manauri ended his tale, silence fell, interrupted only after a long time by Coneso. His eyes shining ominously, the chief addressed Manauri and me in a sharp voice:

"And what gifts have you brought for us?"

Both the sudden hostility and the unexpected words seemed to us incomprehensible. We didn't know what to answer.

"What are you plotting?!" boomed Coneso suddenly.

That was the first time I saw Manauri burst into anger. His face darkened, its features changed, making him almost unrecognizable, and he flashed the scowl of a predatory cat. But he did not lose control of himself. He didn't explode, he didn't make an insane move. He just said in a choked voice:

"How dare you say such words to us? There is no plot.

Remember this, Coneso! We arrive as your bothers, brothers visiting brothers. Our hearts are pure, our thoughts are kind."

"Your hearts are pure?"

"You doubt it? What happened to your famous wisdom? Yes! Our hearts are pure! "

At this, Coneso snorted with hateful laughter.

"And what happened when you visited the Warao? Will you deny that?"

"And what happened when we visited the Warao, Coneso? What are you talking about?"

"Will you deny it? Did you not plot together? Did you not collude?"

"Collude? The Warao welcomed us hospitably, that is all."

"And you did not make a wicked pact?"

"Wicked?"

"Yes, Manauri. A wicked covenant against me, to destroy me, to sow discord in the tribe with the help of the Warao."

This was too much for Manauri. He rose from his stool. Slowly, as if readying to leap, he approached the chief, leaned over him with an expression of contemptuous indignation, and then threw an insult in his face:

"Coneso! Worms have eaten your brain! You are cheap and stingy; you did not offer us enough *kashiri*, nor did you drink any, but you are talking nonsense like a drunk!"

Everyone froze in horror.

The chief of a South American Indian tribe is usually not possessed of absolute power, nor has he the power of life and death over his people. He only rules over them as long as they recognize and admire his bravery and wit. This is why Manauri's insulting words could have had incalculable consequences and might even have led to a catastrophe. After all, Coneso could order his retinue, armed to the teeth, to attack us, who had almost no weapons on us at the moment, and wipe us out in one fell swoop. I thought Manauri had taken things too far.

But there was no fight. Coneso did nothing. He remained sitting still. Perhaps he was afraid of the mood of the tribe? Maybe he wasn't naturally prone to violence?

I realized that the quarrel had to be settled as soon as possible and not allowed to blow up. Yet, I suspected that Manauri, damned dog, had deliberately exacerbated the quarrel in order to test his influence among his tribesmen, and by showing open hostility to Coneso, force a test of strength. If that's what he had aimed for, he had certainly accomplished his aim, but hot heads had to be cooled immediately.

Among a universal commotion, I stood up, and I demanded to speak. Arnak and Vagura seconded me and silenced the people.

"I am a friend of Manauri," I announced in a loud voice. "But I want to be a friend of Coneso, Carapana, and Pirokai, too."

Then I went on to say how, through our shared fate and common struggle, we had come to love and trust each other, the Arawaks, the Africans, and myself, and how sincerely I had come to love my Arawak comrades. They have earned my respect, for I have discovered in them those virtues of heart and mind which I appreciated the most: honesty and loyalty. Because a lie would not pass my lips, Coneso had to believe what I said to him. We arrived with pure intentions, as brothers to brothers, and the covenant offered to us by the Warao was in no way directed against Coneso.

"Then why did you make that pact?" growled Coneso.

"Do you not know what threatens us from the south? Has not a group of Arawak hunters gone missing without a trace?" I reminded him.

Coneso was well aware of the danger posed by the Akawaio, as did all the Arawaks present, and a murmur of understanding passed through the crowd.

"The Warao live not only on the Orinoco," I went on, "but many of their clans live far south, and they have taken beatings from the Akawaio. Is it any surprise that having heard of our martial accomplishments and seen our weapons, they turned to us for help?

What can possibly be wrong with us promising to come to their aid?”

“Then why did they go to you for help and not come to me?” challenged Coneso.

“Because we happened to pass by their settlements. Now, the covenant we made involves all Arawaks on the Imataca, us and you. We are only your representatives, and we now convey to you, Coneso, your alliance with the Warao.”

Even this explanation did satisfy the chief’s wounded vanity.

“And what is this new clan you have formed?” he snorted angrily. “You intend to drive a wedge into the tribe, break us up?”

“God forbid!” I objected energetically. “Any people who have suffered so many years in captivity, have grown accustomed to danger and misfortune, have won their freedom together—such people will want to live together as one family. Do you blame them? And yet, we want to serve the whole tribe!”

“But you bring all kinds of treasure! You will use it to attract others to your lineage! You will create your own tribe! You threaten...”

“Stop, Coneso! Stop!” a drawn-out, senile voice broke in. It was a small, low voice, and yet, what an impression it made! Coneso not only fell silent but, as if in the blink of an eye—cooled down. That was Carapana, the sorcerer, speaking. After his words, there came complete and total silence, as if all stopped breathing.

“Stop!” repeated Carapana. “You bark like a foolish dog!”

Coneso fell silent like a dog indeed, a dog that had just been kicked. His eyes filled with such astonishment that it was not difficult to guess that he had lost all train of thought. He opened his mouth as if wanting to object, but Carapana cut him off:

“These are our brothers! Welcome them!”

“Of course, we are your brothers!” I confirmed, relieved.

“Now, shake their hands!” the sorcerer encouraged the elders. “That is what white people do, and they have long been among the whites. Go and shake hands: Coneso. And you, Pirokai. And all of you!”

The hostile mood vanished as if wiped away with a hand.

Reason and kindness returned. The elders approached us. We exchanged handshakes. Smiles were not spared, nor were kind words lacking. Many of the Indians who had stood aside, scandalized by the moods of their elders, now became visibly relieved.

Only Carapana, the cause of the glorious reconciliation, took no part in the general welcome. He remained sitting on his stool, full of aloof dignity. He smoked his pipe and, from behind the clouds of smoke, studied us carefully, not saying another word.

"We have wondered whether you have brought us gifts from the Warao!" one of the elders said.

"Of course we did," replied Manauri eagerly.

"I want a sword!" shouted Fujudi.

"And I, too, want a sword!" Pirokai seconded him eagerly. And others followed him:

"And me!... And me!..."

Apparently, since our stay with the Warao, Spanish swords had come into fashion on the Orinoco. Alas, we only had two spare swords left, so Coneso and Pirokai got one each. Others contented themselves with clothes and hats, and more than one put on a Spanish caftan. The sorcerer's eyes flashed with greed as he received his gift: a magnificent captain's hat with a beautiful ostrich feather. All the elders were seized by a veritable feeding frenzy. Everyone pestered us with childlike importunity and wanted to be given something, and not just one thing, but many things.

"Give me a matchlock!" Coneso demanded.

"And me, too!" jumped in Pirokai.

"No," I said. "I will not give you guns. I need them, and you can't use them. You will get your guns later."

"When?" the chief pursed his lips in disappointment. "Then give me that captive, the Spaniard!"

"No," I said. "He is my property. I will not give him up."

My second refusal angered him, which did not escape the sorcerer's attention.

"Coneso!" resounded Carapana's sharp warning.

The chief immediately calmed down but continued to look around hungrily. He saw Lasana. His eyes blazed at her sight. His tongue slipped out of his mouth to lick his lips. The chief looked in this one moment simultaneously like a spoiled child and a dissolute savage.

Then his eye fell on our horse, standing nearby.

"I want that horse!" he shouted, throwing me a defiant look, convinced that I would refuse him that precious gift also. But he was mistaken. This time, I did not refuse:

"The horse? You can keep it."

Coneso was struck dumb, amazement painted all over his face: a horse was an extremely rare and priceless animal on the Orinoco.

"I shall give you the horse under one condition!" I added. "Until the day I leave you, I may use it as I please."

Both the unexpected gift and still more my announcement of my imminent departure sobered him up. He looked at me suspiciously.

"You will not stay with us forever?" he asked incredulously.

"I have never intended to do so," I said.

With what extraordinary tension did Carapana listen to our conversation! He positively leaned forward to hear our words better.

"You will not stay?" repeated Coneso surprised. "And when are you going to leave us?"

"I still don't know. At the right time. Perhaps in a few weeks."

"And where will you go?"

"Have you not heard of the English factories in the South, somewhere at the mouth of the Essequibo?"

"I have heard. Will you go there?"

"Yes. I will go there if you help me."

Coneso and Carapana exchanged fleeting glances, but I could not grasp the meaning of that communication. Yet, I felt sure that they were glad to hear that they would soon be rid of me from the Imataca.

"They are afraid of me," I thought.

The day was leaning towards the evening. It was still broad

daylight, but the sun hid behind dark rain clouds gathering over the western horizon. Nearby, the jungle suddenly came alive, simply, as it does in the tropics every day in the late afternoon. And with what passion did the forest come to life, with what wonderful, strange, beautiful voices! When I heard the unknown birds of this new forest sending me their alluring greetings from the thicket, I was suddenly seized with such a hunting fever that I wanted to break away from my party and run into the forest with my fowling piece in hand. If there were so many birds here, how much other game would there be!

Our arduous journey was at an end—at least for my companions, who had reached their goal. They were now among their own people. Many months—hell, many years!—of longing and dreaming have finally come to fruition. We even overcame the last difficulties, shook off the sour welcome of the tribal elders, and disarmed them with sincere words and gifts. So, when the feeding frenzy, the festival of greed, died down, yielding to the joyful buzz of people getting reacquainted, of finding laughter and companionship, I experienced the blissful peace of a soldier after a victorious battle. At last, I could ease off, relax, be myself, let go of my wearisome vigilance before men, and direct my vigilance—ah, a different, reassuring vigilance!—at animals. How the forest smelled again! How sweetly the forest voices played for me! How they lured me into the boiling lushness of the jungle! I had passed my happiest days in Virginia backwoods, gun in hand, hunting, reveling in the charms of the wilderness. Oh, to track a jaguar! To discover new, unknown creatures—this seemed to me a pleasure worth living for.

"Yes!" I thought, and I—daydreamed.

I suddenly came to note the sorcerer's intense gaze. He stared at me, studying me with an unpleasant, mocking smile wandering about his cold lips. When our eyes met, the cruelty of his face immediately disappeared as if hiding itself. With a gesture of his hand, he asked whether I would like to take a sip from his pipe. I gestured back: "Yes."

"Do not take the pipe to your lips!" I suddenly heard a

frightened whisper.

This was our lame Arasibo, sitting on the ground just behind me, warning me in a hushed voice. Nobody heard him but me. But since he spoke Arawak, I pretended not to understand the warning.

I took the pipe from Carapana's hands, put it to my lips, and took a long drag. And in that instant, horrified, I realized the accuracy of the warning. But it was already too late. The pipe contained poison. Through the tobacco smoke, I sensed a foreign, bitter taste. At the same time, my head began to spin, the figure of Carapana swirled before my eyes, and I half passed out. Fortunately, I was sitting on my jaguar skin, or I would have fallen to the ground. All this happened with lightning speed. The weakness lasted only a few seconds, no more, and when I regained consciousness, I saw the sorcerer still smiling at me with the same mocking grimace as before.

My head was still buzzing, but the momentary weakness disappeared almost immediately, and the poison seemed to leave no permanent effects.

Carapana, with excessive politeness, took the pipe from my hand and inhaled it himself once, twice, and a third time, sucking in and then blowing out copious clouds of smoke. I watched him attentively, his slightest movement not escaping my eyes. But, though the sorcerer changed nothing in the pipe and smoked like the devil, I saw no signs of weakness in him. On him, the poison did not work, or, more likely, it wasn't in the smoke at all when he smoked, though I couldn't explain to myself how that was possible.

Carapana, seeing my amazement, chuckled, amused, and taunted me:

"You are not used to the tobacco from our parts, it seems to me."

I rose. My knees were still bending under me. I leaned over the sorcerer, frowned menacingly, and, showing him my fist, I drawled:

"Listen, Carapana. I tell you this for your own good: you do not want to know me otherwise than as your good friend. I recommend you put aside your stupid tricks."

Carapana ignored these words—translated by Arnak—as if they had not reached his mind. He apparently thought the whole thing was a good joke. A sense of triumph beamed from his eyes when, with a sneer and pretended compassion, he excused himself:

"Our tobacco does not agree with you!"

Clearly, the whole incident had been intended as a warning, and that's how I understood it. And, sadly, I realized that that vigilance against fellow men, that vigilance I had been so eager to leave behind, could not be let go of. I did not dare avert my watchful eye from my fellow men.

Venomous Snakes

The poison inflicted on me by the sorcerer did not cause me any serious ailment, and half an hour later, I was fully recovered. When we were alone, Arasibo, speaking through Arnak, explained the sorcerer's trick to me. Namely, in his bamboo pipe, there were two pipes separated by a wooden plate: one contained ordinary tobacco, the other—tobacco mixed with poison. When one held the pipe in his hand, one could squeeze it surreptitiously, unobserved by others, and thus close the poisoned tube and inhale only the smoke of the safe tobacco. Those who did not know the trick inhaled the smoke from both tubes and lost consciousness.

"Is it a strong poison?" I asked.

"And how!" Arasibo assured us. "Had you taken more, you would have died."

"And how do you know all this?" I looked at Arasibo with admiration.

The invalid, pleasantly flattered, smiled from ear to ear:

"I have watched him! I have spied! I have taught myself his magic and his ways!"

"This is why they hate Arasibo," interjected Arnak.

"Carapana and Coneso?"

"Yes! If they could, they would strangle him!"

The hut assigned to me by the chief stood near the river, over half a mile from the hut of Coneso, and several dozen paces away stood the shack where Manauri was to live for the time being.

When, on the following morning, after having slept at night on board our schooner, I went down to my hut to inspect it, the first thing I saw inside was—a human skull placed against the wall on a mound of earth. The abomination bared its teeth at everyone who entered.

I shuddered at the eerie sight and immediately summoned my companions. Overwhelmed with horror, they stood speechless for a while and then nodded their heads vigorously.

"A man died here," Arnak explained to me. "And this is his grave and his skull. Caribs bury their dead in the huts where they lived."

"You say this is a Carib? Was this not an Arawak hut?"

"No. This hut is very old, and some Caribs must have lived here. No one living dares to remain in such a hut except the spirit of the deceased."

"So why did Coneso assign this hut to me?" I asked, surprised.

"Maybe he supposes," said Arnak, "that this custom is important to us but not to you, white people."

"I don't think so," grumbled Manauri.

We took counsel together and decided that I should not live in a hut with a grave. Staying in that hut was really not to my taste, but chiefly, it could alienate many Indians as a sacrilege and scare them away.

So I moved into Manauri's hut, and with the help of many local volunteers, my companions and I set about building a new shelter for me. Work went briskly and cheerfully, and by noon, I had a house, not much poorer than the residence of Coneso himself, a house with a strong roof of palm fronds, resistant to storms, with three bamboo walls, and the fourth partly uncovered, and protected from downpours by outspread eaves. The house was so spacious that Arnak and Vagura, my inseparable friends, and Pedro all moved into it as well.

The rest of our companions built similar huts for themselves in great haste, but not in dispersal as Indians usually did, but all together, crowding one another. Our clan really wanted to remain together, and our feelings found their expression in this work. Our Africans all stationed themselves quite close to Manauri's hut, like a chief's bodyguard, whereas Arasibo preferred to settle at my side and be my nearest neighbor, while on the other side, just as close to my hut, settled Lasana with her child.

When Coneso visited us in the evening to see how we had arranged ourselves, I took the opportunity to give him a few words of the bitter truth about the hut with the dead man. I told him unequivocally that I have a vengeful nature, do not bear insults lightly, and do not always forgive wrongs done to me.

"Wrongs?" asked the rogue pretending surprise. "There was no harm here!"

"No harm? Then what was it? A ridiculous prank? Or a malicious trap?"

"Maybe a prank," he seemed to admit playfully, and his fleshy lips formed an unpleasant smile. "But not malicious. It was a test of your strength!"

"One man wishing to test me treats me to a poisonous pipe and another to a hut with a ghost! What kind of 'tests' are these?"

"Does that surprise you?" his mouth smiled again, but his steely eyes remained cold, lurking.

"Yes, it does surprise me. I am a guest in your village, Coneso."

"Yes, you are a guest, but an unusual guess. We don't know you. They say you have great power. We're just trying to test it!"

"Which is why you give me poison?"

"Exactly! We wanted to know if poison affects you. Now we know it does. Then we wanted to test your spirit, and now we know that the spirit of the deceased is stronger than you! You are afraid of him!"

"In this, you are wrong, Coneso!"

"But didn't you flee from the forbidden hut?"

"Oh, yes, I did—and how! But not for the reasons you think."

"Oh?" he twisted his lips in mocking disbelief.

"I respect your customs and beliefs," I insisted. "I do not want to insult your dead."

But doubt remained in his eyes as he inspected me head to toe unashamedly:

"People say that matchlock bullets bounce off you."

"Nonsense!"

"And that arrows shot from an ordinary bow cannot pierce your skin. Is this true?"

"Foolishness!" I was not joking. "I am as mortal as the rest of you. It is with me as it is with every one of you."

Coneso's gaze remained suspicious: he did not believe me. He tilted his head distrustfully and shook it from side to side.

"But you will not deny that there is something in you that others do not have?"

"That much is true."

"You see?"

He said this with triumph in his voice, but I immediately put it out:

"There's something in me that you do not have. More experience. I have traveled much of the world and encountered many enemies. Some I beat, others beat me. And from the latter, I learned the most. I learned. You hear? That is my special power!"

"And when did you meet a jaguar?" he asked in a changed voice, thinking this question ambushed me.

I replied nonchalantly:

"I met a jaguar once. I met him on an uninhabited island.

Arnak, Vagura, and I killed him.

"That was the jaguar king!" murmured Coneso significantly.

"The devil knows him."

"And did the jaguar then come to you in a dream?" holding his breath, the chief asked like an examining judge.

"Oh, yes!" I snorted out loud, laughing. "I dreamed about jaguars many times after killing that one! And do you dream?"

"I do," he grunted. "But my dreams are different. They are wholesome."

We had the conversation in front of my hut, in the shade of its extended eave, and I didn't really know whether his doubts had been resolved. I rather thought that they weren't.

Then we saw Lasana, returning from the river, carrying a large gourd of water on her head. At the sight of the pretty woman, Coneso's eyes widened with lust, and he looked as if he wanted to devour her alive.

"Why are you here?" he exclaimed to her, surprised.

"I live here," she answered curtly and went past us, paying him no more attention.

"Lasana! Stop!" he called after her. "I wish to say something to you. This is not your place!"

"And where is my place?" she stared him in the face and slowed down her stride.

"You belong in my hut!" he declared. "Go there right now!"

Lasana threw him a not-very-polite glance but was unable to hide her fear completely.

"Did you fall and hurt your head?" she huffed.

"Don't get too uppity girl. I say, go to my hut."

"I will not go to your hut," she said firmly. "Not now and not ever. I belong to the clan of the White Jaguar, and this is my place. I live here."

"You will do as I say!" the chief raised his voice sharply. "Go! Move!"

Her resistance angered him. Clearly, he liked her and hoped to possess her.

"Wait, Coneso!" I interjected with the softest, friendliest voice I could muster and touched his arm.

"Let's talk calmly like normal people do. Arawak women have their rights and are not slaves of men. That's what people have told me."

"What's this?" Coneso brushed off my hand brusquely.

"I am saying that she has the right to do as she likes."

"No. Not quite. She is young. She had a husband, and she lost him. She has a child. The tribe has a responsibility to look after her."

"She already has a guardian."

"Who?"

"Me."

Coneso narrowed his eyes:

"Do you want to say that you are her husband? I know you are not!"

"I am not her husband. But I am entrusted with her care."

"And she wanted this care?"

"I did!" Lasana confirmed in a loud voice, belligerently shaking her head. "I asked for it, and I still want it!"

We were not alone. Apart from Arnak, a dozen Indians from our group and a few local Arawaks stood about witnessing the scene.

Especially the latter seemed scandalized by Coneso's brazen demand. The chief noticed this and decided to avoid further confrontation.

"We will see about this," he muttered under his nose and turned to leave.

"Listen, Coneso!" I stopped him. "The situation is clear for all to see. Lasana will stay here, by me. But what you say is unclear and confusing."

"What do you mean?"

"You keep affronting us. Why? Have you not received a horse and a sword from us? Is that not enough for you?"

"You are right! Maybe that was not enough!" he said and he

laughed at his own joke.

"There's something I don't understand," I went on. "Over there somewhere in the south, the Akawaio are readying for a war against us, but you, our chief and commander at war, instead of focusing our vigilance and strength, instead of doing everything you can to unite the tribe and prepare us for defense, you waste your time and energy like a blind madman, virulent and quarrelsome, on spreading discord in your tribe. Listen to me, and listen carefully: you are bringing a storm on yourself and a misfortune on all of us."

"Who?" exclaimed Coneso, as if amused. "Who is doing this? I? I spread discord?"

"Who else?"

"You! Before you came, no one violated the harmony of the tribe. Who demolished our peace? You are to blame for everything!"

And thus, blaming us for his own behavior, he turned around and walked off.

A serious dilemma now lay before us. Some of my friends, the more impatient and less inclined to compromise, proposed that we all leave Serima immediately and set up our own settlement on the Imataca a few miles above the inhospitable village, but most, including Manauri, opposed it. They believed that the bad mood of the elders would go away eventually, and all the misunderstandings would soon cease.

Days passed in rest and idleness.

We had plenty of food, for the inhabitants of Serima, well settled in the area, generously shared their supplies with us and allowed us to go to the fields and harvest their ripe crops. Our food staple was the enormous root of a plant called by the Indians *mandioca*,[4] from which the indigestible juice had to be pressed before the tubers were boiled and eaten. Numerous fruits, both cultivated and wild, added variety to our diet, as did fish, of which huge shoals swarmed in the

---

[4] Cassava

river and in almost every puddle. In addition, of course, we never neglected game, from wild pigs to caterpillars nesting in rotten trunks.

Within a few days, our people settled into the daily routine of an Indian village. While some looked for suitable sections of the forest where we could clear the trees and begin to farm, others went out on the water to fish in different ways, now with a rod, now with a trap, now by blocking off a stream or shooting with a bow, or even killing fish with poison. Still others went to the forest to pick fruit or hunt game. I accompanied the last group, happy to be in my element at last.

We brought the schooner closer to our settlement and anchored it opposite my cabin. The idea was to keep the ship close and under constant watch, for we stored in its hatches our provisions and various other goods captured from the Spanish. The thought of the Akawaio did not let me rest, and I led firearms practice several times. The gunners were eager to practice, making me proud, and when they got the hang of it, I let them take fowling pieces along on the hunt. They found their own bows and arrows more useful for the purpose, but they zealously took their guns along and strapped them over their shoulders since, clearly, in their eyes, guns aided male sex appeal and increased personal dignity.

In moments free from these expeditions, we took up exercises with other weapons—bows, spears, clubs, and the as yet unknown to me blowpipe: a bamboo pipe eight or nine feet long, from which little poisoned darts could be blown to a great distance. We all fell into a kind of competitive fever, and some shooters were astonishingly good at it.

Coneso and his henchman Pirokai tried to break up our group from the very beginning by luring people away with rich promises, but they achieved little. Their efforts, with the exception of two wavering souls, proved in vain. Our people wanted to be together. We really felt like a clan, a family, and I soon realized what it was about: not only the common experience of shared misery and danger, not only the presence of their English friend with his guns and his rich ship, but above all, the feeling that they were different from other Arawaks.

Tried by fate, proven in action, they had hardened, they became hardier, possessed as it were, thicker blood, greater vitality. They were more resilient, more mobile, more curious about the things of the world, more thirsty for the joy of life than their local countrymen.

Their resourcefulness and ingenuity also had a magical influence on many of the inhabitants of Serima. These Indians, usually lethargic and sluggish in spirit, now seemed to wake up and think more broadly. It was understandable that several of the immediate family of the various members of the White Jaguar Clan had come to live with us. But others, by no means only relatives, also flocked to our group, attracted by some irresistible force. How they craved our friendship, sought our advice and our cheerful chat, how willingly they would settle permanently somewhere close to our campfires. However, Manauri strongly objected to it, not wishing to anger Coneso and his allies.

We went hunting in twos or threes. I usually went with Arnak, Vagura, or Pedro, and sometimes with Lasana after she moved to her hut. And now I experienced the incredible, astonishing thing that our jungle was. In the north, my native Virginia forest was full of all sorts of trees, but what was that to the mad luxury, to the unbridled variety of plants here? I was used to the Virginia thicket, but how to compare it with this wild tangle, this green fury, this mass of inexorable branches, leaves, vines, thorns, where it was difficult to take a step, where everything imprisoned a man, weighed down his body, suffocated his mind and soul? Yet, when you experienced it more closely and regarded it carefully, this mindless, mind-numbing confusion revealed its internal logic and order, and this made me see the jungle's wild beauty and take profound pleasure in it. But I never knew what the jungle was to me or to any man: was it a kind friend or an implacable enemy?

There were many animals in this forest, but they were difficult to spot and even harder to hunt. A green veil covered them, and at the same time, their alert senses warned them from afar of the approach of a hunter. Yet, in this wilderness, there were paths, both human and animal, and they made it possible to sneak quietly and approach the game.

If the great fascination of hunting is the surprise that awaits the hunter behind every bush, and the source of its magic is the possibility of an unforeseen development, then the forest of Imataca could be called the perfect hunting ground, a hunter's paradise, a cradle of all unlikely encounters. What varied beasts ran through this forest, what wonders wandered here!

In addition to the jaguar, other predatory cats might jump out in front of the hunter, one of which, as fawn-colored as a lion, Pedro called a *puma*. *Guasupita* deer and wild *saguino* pigs in the depths of the woods, water pigs on the banks of the rivers, and *mashadis*, huge animals with skin as hard as a shield and noses elongated like a bizarre elephant trunk. And monkeys. Countless flocks of monkeys. Or, one could encounter *hateke*—a beast completely covered with armor plate, and another freak, *tamanoa*, a devourer of ants with a ridiculously long snout and front claws so robust that it could tear a man apart, or meet an even greater freak, *unau*, a quadruped completely docile, hanging like fruit under a tree branch and, all the more surprising, almost motionless.

And a variety of water and forest turtles and lizards, among which the *iguana* were real dragons, both in appearance and disposition, only more modest in size; and a numerous tribe of venomous snakes and giant constrictor snakes, and the treacherous caymans—crocodiles lurking in still waters. And in these waters, apart from the swarms of edible fish, what monsters: the flat *sipari* with a poisonous spike in the tail, the small *huma* of maddening bloodthirstiness, *jaringa*, the Indian stories about which at first seemed to me a fairy tale, because the little monsters, quite unassuming to look at, when touched by a man supposedly struck him with a thunderbolt and paralyzed him. And the immeasurable, colorful world of millions of birds on the ground and in the air, a world garrulous, gorgeous, cheerful, above which, however, circled the gloomy ruler of the sky: the crested giant eagle, the semi-legendary *mezime*, the invincible killer of monkey, a giant said to be able to lift a fifteen-year-old boy into the air.

The Arawaks, who had been living on Imataca for two years, did not hide from me what they knew about the secrets of the forest, so I heard a lot about many strange things. It was sometimes difficult to tell where the truth ended and the imagination began because they warned me with equal trepidation of the danger of the jaguar and the malice of the *kanaima*, which I already knew was a vengeful spirit and with equal plasticity described to me the wonderful form of the vicious *iguana* as the appearance of the forest *hebu*—hairy creatures with protruding eyes, beings that turned out to be malicious spirits of the dead. Right after they described to me dramatic cases of attack on men by the great snake *komuti*, which did indeed live by the water's edge, they told me with equal alacrity about the *maikisikiri*—water creatures, which appeared only to women, never to men, and were cruelly obsessed with the female sex—and only later did I learn that *maikisikiri* were water spirits. And thus, the real world and the fantastic interpenetrated each other in a head-spinning wrestling match, and entering the boundless forest, I never knew where the limits of danger lay, the boundary of horror and delight, reality and delusion. This feeling of uncertainty filled me with a strange and immeasurable delight—like everything in this forest.

Near our huts dwelled a great profusion of disgusting reptiles and many venomous snakes, especially near the path leading from our huts to the forest. We killed several a day, but always, on the following morning, there was no sign of depletion among them, and we found new monsters crawling on the ground.

"Well, they sure love us!" I said playfully. "Are they falling from the sky?"

My friends looked at each other perplexed, supposedly in some absurd sense of guilt or shame for this disfavor of nature.

They explained to me that sometimes it happened like that: you didn't find a viper's tail in one area and a whole swarm elsewhere. Manauri recalled how once, many years ago, he had come into a glade where a dozen snakes were basking in the sun, and they were all *sororoima*, too, the most poisonous of the poisonous. He managed to escape unscathed, but for days, his skin tingled at the memory.

So, having no other recourse, I made my peace with my high Spanish boots and wore them for safety, for the teeth of serpents could not pierce their leather. And Lasana's mother, an extremely kind woman and well disposed towards me, helped in her own way: she brought me a tame *thuiuiu*, a huge stork with a black head and beak, a zealous exterminator of all reptiles. And with his arrival, the plague was much reduced along the path.

It became a habit for me to visit the schooner each morning and to go down the hatch, where we kept the powder kegs, and make sure all was in order. And a piebald mongrel, our cheerful guardian and watchdog, usually ran up the plank with me, wagging his tale good-naturedly.

Once, the dog jumped down the hatch ahead of me, growled piteously, and immediately jumped out in total terror. Chasing after him came out a small snake, dark and bronze dappled. Venomous, as I guessed immediately from the shape of his head. I barely managed to dodge him. Luckily, I held a cudgel in my hand. I serviced the reptile once and again, then threw him overboard. But there was another snake in the hatch, just as dangerous, and I soon discovered a third under the helm. This one curled up in a ball and lifted its head, ready to strike at me, rage blazing in his tiny eyes. I easily dealt with all three monsters, for they could not move fast on deck and were really only dangerous when approached by an unsuspecting man. But I became puzzled: there was no natural explanation for their presence on the ship. The schooner was surrounded by water on all sides and had no connection with land except when the gangplank was lowered. So, where did the scary reptiles come from? Were they planted by someone who knew my ways and hoped to kill me? The matter was strange, and the reptiles—terrifying.

The dog, barely scratched by the first snake, did not live to see the shore again. He suddenly fell, paralyzed, and lived another minute, maybe two. Terrible convulsions shook his body, and a bloody foam formed at his mouth. Then, he began to bleed through his eyes and ears. When all his movement ceased, I understood the deadly effect of the venom, and, at the same time, I realized that had my guardian not gone ahead of me, I'd be lying lifeless in his place.

Generally, I don't scare easily, but I shivered with horror standing on the bridge. Though I did not share my suspicions with my friends, they were quick to guess whose hand was behind the mysterious plague of snakes. Whose? It didn't take a genius to guess. And now the strange abundance of snakes along our path also appeared inexplicable no more.

"Yes, it's him. It's his doing!" said Arnak, frowning, and looked around as if searching in the thickets for the hidden enemy.

"Oh, he's not there now," I smiled ruefully. "I guess he brings the reptiles at night."

"You think he drops them here?" asked Manauri doubtfully.

"And who would it be if not Carapana?" I asked, surprised.

"Oh, yes, he is behind this, no doubt. But does he bring them himself?"

"If not he, then one his helpers."

"I am not sure this is the case."

"Well, how do they get here, then? Fly?"

Deep anxiety flashed on Manauri's face.

"He is a sorcerer," he murmured as if that explained anything.

"And he uses magic to lure those beasts?" I asked.

"Perhaps he can! He is a great, dangerous sorcerer!" Manauri replied evasively.

I now realized that the chief associated the appearance of these serpents with evil sorcery, and so did others, all with the exception of Arnak. Sorcery is a great power in the Indian mind, and it is hopeless to fight it. I became anxious that my Arawak friends would abandon me to a *force majeure*—a power they could not hope to oppose—or at least become discouraged. But it soon turned out that they had no intention of abandoning me or even letting their spirits down, and all for a reason they promptly revealed to me: Carapana was formidable, but I was *Paranakedi*—an Englishman—and a White Jaguar to boot, and therefore I had my own witchcraft not worse than the most powerful of sorcerers.

"So, you think I can take him?" I asked.

"Easy," they replied.

"I prefer to oppose him with a surer method than witchcraft!"

"Oh, but there is no better method!" shouted several Indians at once. "What other method can you use?"

"Vigilance."

Contemptuous dismissal flickered in their faces.

"Well, yes, naturally, but..."

"But will you help me?"

"Of course! How could we not? You are our White Jaguar! Our friend!" they assured me.

"Very well. We will take our guns and wait in ambush for the scoundrel at night. We will match his magic with our bullets, and we will see which is stronger."

However, this they did not like. The idea of going out at night and, what's more, *shooting*, too, upset them. They did not want to challenge the powers that dwelt in the night. At night, they preferred to sleep rather than hunt some terrible unknown. All they had to do was increase their vigilance and exterminate the snakes more diligently.

When, on the following day, at dawn, I went hunting with Pedro and Arnak, at the point where the path entered the forest, we stopped suddenly. Across the path, as if blocking our way, lay several tiny sculptures made from clay, awkwardly, as if made by a child's hand. The moment he spotted them, Arnak crouched down and, with a violent movement of his hands, stopped us from going any further. With a stupor on his face, so unusual for him, he stared at the figurines.

No more than a finger or a finger and a half in size, they represented various animals, such as a lizard, a tiny toad, a young snake, some four-legged animal, a bird, and even a scorpion. All the creatures were positioned so that they turned their heads towards us, and upon

A Caribbean King
Christoph Weigel after Caspar Luyken
Neu-eröffnete Welt-Galleria, Nürnberg 1703

closer inspection, I noticed that each one showed a hideous distortionin some body part: one had a flattened head, one a severed paw, one a broken back and gouged out eyes.

"Do not come closer," whispered Arnak. I looked at my friend, surprised and a little flustered by his reaction.

"What? Witchcraft again?" I asked nonchalantly.

"Yes, witchcraft!" he confirmed.

"And you allow yourself to be tricked? Arnak! My dear Arnak. This is horseshit."

"No, it's not horseshit," he denied. "It's not nonsense anymore! If a sorcerer wants to destroy someone, he puts such enchanted figurines in his path.".

"Whatever for?"

"In order to weaken him, frighten him, confuse him..."

"Ha! Well, I am not confused!" I declared and stepped forward to crush the figurines.

"Don't do this! They could be poisoned, and the poison could penetrate through your boots!"

After a moment, Arnak cooled down, his forehead cleared, and a slight smile appeared on his lips.

"No, Yan!" he said more cheerfully, as if to appease me. "You have taught me well that this is superstition and that it has no power. But I don't like it because it clearly shows that Carapana hates you and wants to destroy you. And that thought bothers me."

"How do you know he wants to destroy me in particular and not all of us?"

"Look!"

He pointed out a place several steps behind the row of figurines, and there I saw on the path yet another statuette of an animal.

The carving represented a cat—a jaguar painted white and, therefore, a white jaguar. Ah, that was clearly me. A tiny spear pierced the beast's chest—apparently, this fate was destined for me as well. All these threats with figurines only made me shrug, and yet there was some ferocity, a profoundly hateful intent in this whole project, and it appeared to me amazing. Was I beginning to succumb to the pernicious influence of the sorcerer?

Meanwhile, Arnak broke off a branch, and he started to lay into the statuettes with all his might until he smashed them to bits and swept the pieces carefully from the path. He intended to do the same with the statuette of the jaguar, but I stopped him, wanting to keep it as a keepsake. The boy shook his head disapprovingly but agreed.

"Just be careful," he warned me, "and do not touch it!"

So we tied it up with thin lianas and hung it on a bush to collect it on the way back.

A few hours later, when we returned by the same path, a new surprise awaited us: the statuette had disappeared. Someone stole it while we hunted. No one in our clan did it. It followed that a stranger was lurking about our huts. The forest surrounding us like a wall hid within its womb a somber mystery, and we were helpless against its opaque tangle.

"The enemy has a white jaguar with a pierced heart!" Arnak said. "Be careful about your heart!"

"My heart is as healthy as a horse," I snorted.

And it was true: my health served me well. It positively gushed. It did surprise me, for the bogs we have crossed must have housed innumerable diseases, the best proof of which were my Indians: many of them were wasted by various fevers and other vile ailments. But I was as healthy as a bear.

On the second or third night after the discovery of the ominous carvings, I slept poorly, and when I woke up, I could not go back to sleep. The usual tumultuous music came from the nearby forest, another orchestra shouted from the river, somewhat different, though equally noisy, and some lizards or other vermin rustled in the reed walls of the hut. Sleep fell off my eyes for good, many thoughts knocked about inside my head. The sorcerer, with incomprehensible obstinacy, produced ever more trouble for us and created a steadily less tenable situation. I had to take firm steps. But what?

Suddenly, I froze. My whole being transformed into hearing. I was lying alone, near one of the walls, on a bed of branches covered with skins. And just above me, I heard something that seemed different from all the other sounds about. It sounded like the rustling of straw slowly being pushed aside. After a moment, I became certain that someone standing outside my hut was working a hole in my wall. I was getting ready to jump out and catch the mystery visitor when an object landed on my belly, and I froze. It was fortunate that I did not lose my mind and flinch: it was a snake! Lucky presence of mind saved my life.

The snake wasn't very big, probably no more than a foot and a half. After the fall, it lurked still on my body as if it didn't know what to do next. I barely dared to breathe, and my heart was beating within me like possessed. In recent days, I have had the opportunity to learn the nature of these reptiles through and through, so I was perfectly aware that the slightest movement on my part was enough to irritate the beast, and an irritated snake was ready to slash me with its poisonous tooth.

After a moment, which seemed to last a century, the snake slowly uncoiled and began to slither. I felt his cold, slimy body, and I summoned my whole strength of will not to budge. It slid off my belly but didn't move away. Slowly, it moved along my body and later even coiled about one of my ankles and remained in that position for a few minutes. But I withstood that as well, and the reptile eventually left my bed.

I breathed out. My whole body was covered in cold sweat. Only after some time did my heart calm down, my blood began to circulate normally, and clarity of thought returned.

All this happened in complete darkness, not allowing me to see anything. Although imminent danger no longer threatened me, I knew that I was not yet in the clear. The reptile was somewhere near, perhaps lurking only several inches away. I didn't dare to move, let alone cry out to my companions sleeping in their hammocks.

I spent several hours lying totally still until daybreak. When the light, penetrating through the cracks of my hut, began to disperse the darkness, I carefully looked around. I didn't see the snake anywhere. My companions woke up gradually. I informed them about what had happened. We got up.

After searching every hiding place in the cabin, we finally found the snake. It had not gone far: it had hidden among the branches under my bed. Apparently, it was an extremely venomous and aggressive variety. Cornered, it threw itself at us. We had to work quickly with our clubs to render it harmless.

There was a clearly visible hole in the wall above my bed: clear proof of the crime. We all understood the gravity of the moment and the need for more effective defense than heretofore. Nobody opposed me anymore when I demanded that we post armed sentries at night.

"I will keep watch!" Arasibo was the first to volunteer, hate burning in his eyes.

"We will all take turns!" replied Arnak.

"I'll go first! Tonight!" insisted the invalid.

The man was cross-eyed, and as one needed perfect eyesight at night, I objected, but my friends assured me that Arasibo had cat's eyes and could see very well in the dark. Accordingly, we selected a blunderbuss for him, loaded it with lead shot, and I ordered him not to shoot from a distance closer than thirty paces—to make it less likely that he killed anyone. And to avoid hitting our own, to hail the person before shooting, to confirm it was not one of us.

"Oh, I will find out who he is!" growled Arasibo.

In the evening, we warned our neighbors not to go out at night, especially not on the path leading into the forest.

At about midnight, we were woken up by a loud bang. We grabbed our weapons and jumped out and heard Arasibo yelling that he had shot a man who'd been sneaking about.

"Did you hail him first?" I asked the invalid.

"What for? I knew it was the enemy!"

Hastily, we kindled torches and ran to the place indicated by Arasibo but found nobody there. Our sharpshooter had missed or only barely scratched the visitor or perhaps had hallucinated.

When the day broke, I examined the place once again, and this time I found something. I discovered blood. Arasibo was triumphant: there was a lot of blood.

The Great Serpent and the Wild Jaguar

Arasibo's shot bore very good fruit, for it seemed to scare away malicious spirits. The plague of snakes soon stopped, and no one disturbed our peace at night: we kept nightly vigils in vain. After a few days, the Indians wanted to abandon the vigil, but I did not agree to this, and finally, it was my turn: the dry season, the season of wars, had come to the forest, and our night watch was meant to protect us not against one, but against two dangers at once: the sorcerer's plots and the possibility of an attack by the Akawaio. I had required all the men of our clan to keep watch by turns. Such vigilance was against the nature of my Indians, who had no gift for foreseeing adversity, but I managed to persuade them because they respected me and didn't want to annoy me.

One mystery remained: whom did Arasibo shoot? He hit no one from our clan, nor did he hit Carapana, Coneso, Pirokai, or Fujudi, as we soon learned.

Anticipating trouble with the Akawaio, I wished to have an accurate map of the forests, mountains, rivers, and paths between the lower Orinoco and the Cuyuni River to the south, so I sent Arnak and Pedro, an expert mapmaker, to all the people in Serima who might be able to give more accurate reports of the country. They gave them willingly, and soon a beautiful map was produced, of great use to me, and at the same time, cunning Arnak made careful inquiries as to the mysterious night visitor. And he found nothing: the wounded man disappeared into thin air. If he was lying somewhere healing, he had hidden himself very carefully indeed.

My relations with Pedro were excellent. He turned out to be a cheerful, honest, obliging boy, and it was impossible not to like him. He quickly made friends with Vagura. They became inseparable like brothers, and it seemed at times that Pedro forgot he was in captivity. He was skillful and willing, and he helped me not only with learning Spanish: he was quick to pick up the Arawak language too. He enjoyed the same liberties as all the others. I gave him a gun and promised him that I would return him to his countrymen at the first opportunity. It was a little amusing, but thanks to him, I discovered something very satisfying to me: namely, that among the Spaniards, who were otherwise famous for their cruelty, there were also noble individuals worthy of love and respect.

One morning, I went hunting with Vagura and Lasana. We walked along a path we often used, which, I was told, ran tens of miles south through the gorges of the Imataca Mountains to the valley of the Cuyuni River and had been used since time immemorial by traveling Indian merchants. I had a pistol in my belt and a fowling piece on my shoulder, a shotgun which carried well, if not as far as a musket. Lasana had a bow that seldom missed, and Vagura had armed himself with a weapon little used in this region: a blowpipe. Its darts, small and light, were terrible: they had been tipped in *urari*, a lightning-speed poison, and as little as a scratch from one laid instantly dead whatever it hit, man or beast.

When, after about two hours, we reached an area rich in game, we were caught in such a downpour that it became almost dark in the forest. Lasana and I hid under the canopy of a mighty trunk of a tree called by the Indians *mora*, and Vagura hid himself similarly just a few dozen steps away.

Even though we were in what was called the dry season, we experienced similar torrential rains almost every day, lasting an hour or two, followed by a strong sun and clear sky of the deepest azure.

This time, the downpour did not last long, and within half an hour, the rain stopped, and it became light in the forest again.

We were still standing under our tree when, looking around out of the old hunter's habit, I looked up into the branches of the tree.

Crowded together, there grew three forests here because apart from the usual, high-growing trees, there was the unbroken thicket of bushes foaming at their feet and a third forest growing out of the boughs and branches of the trees above: a whole forest, an army of parasitic bushes, vines, and weeds. And the whole tangle was shrouded in all directions by a mad network of liana-ropes. I stared at this profligacy in blissful astonishment.

Suddenly, I focused my eyesight. My heart beat faster. I brought my fowling piece to my eye to shoot. Only a few paces above us, a mighty serpent lurked in the branches of a tree. It was not the gray *komuti* that lived near the water, for it was vividly colored: it was covered with yellowish blotches on a reddish-gray background. It was impossible to guess how long it was because I could only see part of his body, but judging by the thickness of his torso, it had to be a giant. His head peeked through the leaves of the canopy, and he was looking straight down at us. He had discovered us long ago.

I was still hesitating whether to shoot when our attention was diverted by an unusual noise coming from far away, from the depths of the wilderness. Broken branches crackled here and there, and the noise came closer and closer to us, and then we heard other sounds, too, rough and dull: some like croaking, some like grunting.

"*Saguino!*" Lasana whispered to me. "Wild pigs!"

A whole pack was marching straight at us. I have heard plenty of stories about how dangerous these animals were if one annoyed them carelessly. Blinded by fury, they charged the enemy in a pack, man or jaguar, and no matter how he defended himself, most often, they tore him to death. Only a hasty escape up a tree could save the victim from their enraged jaws.

The lowest branches of the *mora* tree under which we stood grew about ten feet off the ground, so, grabbing Lasana, I lifted her and helped her reach the lowest branch. She climbed up and helped me follow her. We saw that Vagura had also climbed his tree.

I checked my powder, for it sometimes got wet in the forest, and added a little more.

"Look!" Lasana turned her attention to the snake.

The reptile, who had heard the approach of the herd of wild boar as well as we did, now came to life. He slowly lowered his body. His tail, hooked somewhere among the branches above, supported him while the head and the upper part of his body hovered in the air, not too high above the ground. As he hung motionless, more like a thick liana than a snake, he seemed to emanate a hidden horror, some insidious ghastliness, and it was obvious that he schemed something ominous in his flattened head.

Meanwhile, the pack arrived. They glided among the bushes directly below us and around us with an unhurried step. There was a whole swarm of them, maybe a hundred, maybe more—it was hard to see them all in the bush. I waited with shooting so that as many beasts would pass by as possible, but Lasana shot one of the first sows with a bow from a distance of a dozen or so paces. With a shrill snort, the beast bit the arrow with its mouth and broke it off, but it was immediately hit in the neck for the second time and fell down. Snapping furiously, the animal summoned part of the herd to her. The wild pigs surrounded her, and with the bristles on their necks straight up, they raised their heads and scented loudly, but they did not discover us.

And then the snake struck. He grasped the spine of a beast weighing a good two score pounds with his jaws and, as if it were a small bird, lifted him up in the air. The piercing squeal of the captive tore through the air. The snake, ignoring the cries and the desperate wriggles of its prey, heaved itself higher. There, he put it to the trunk of the tree on which we were sitting, no more than ten feet above our heads, and he wrapped both the trunk and the boar with one coil of his body and—squeezed. The hug was deadly.

We heard a crunching sound of snapping ribs. The animal

seemed to puff up a bit and stiffened.

All this took place before the eyes of the pack, who stood spellbound, watching the murder. But already, during the last convulsions of the victim, the wild pigs swung into action. Several of them attacked the tree, hacking at it with their tusks.

The tree was not thick, four man's hands could easily embrace it. The trunk trembled from root up under the pressure of the furious jaws. The snake retreated upwards. The maddened mob below grew more and more furious. Splinters flew from the trunk. With a dull thud, the body of the dead animal fell to the ground. The herd jumped back instantly but immediately went on the attack again with redoubled savagery.

It was obvious that the tree would not last. The snake understood this, too.

Meanwhile, Lasana was not idle. She kept shooting at the animals below, and though not every arrow was deadly, not a single one missed.

Despite the situation and against my better judgment, I could not resist casting brief glances at the woman. Excited, flushed, with her hair flying about her—what a stunning sight she presented!

She sat astride the branch, her sturdy thighs wrapping it in a tight embrace, and the suppleness of her body and the firmness of her arms were a thing of wonder and beauty. The action below and the excitement of the hunt carried me away as much as the handsome creature next to me, and yet old memories forced themselves upon my feverish mind: when once, as a boy, I had seen a drawing in my father's house representing the naked Roman goddess, Diana, as she shot a deer with a bow. The image made an indelible impression on me then, and now I remember it clearly.

Finally, I decided to start shooting myself. I let out at the pigs with my fowling piece, and though the animals did hear the rumble overhead, they were so enraged, so blinded by their fury, that they could think only of the serpent and went at the tree with wild abandon. I loaded the shotgun calmly and ripped into the pack again and again with good success.

The serpent realized that his refuge, shaken to its very foundation, would soon fall. Nearby stood other trees, whose branches intertwined with the branches of our tree. Unfortunately for the serpent, all were quite limp and could not bear the weight of the snake's body. But there were lianas hanging like garlands from tree to tree, connecting neighboring trunks, and some were quite thick. And the snake chose one of them as his means of escape.

It chose badly. For, while the vine was thick and strong and unbreakable, it was only loosely attached to the opposite trunk. The snake, advancing with all caution, had not yet reached the middle of the liana when the thing, under the snake's enormous weight, began to slide down gradually. The wild pigs below, seeing this, let out a hellish scream and started jumping up to reach the enemy. They didn't reach it: the snake was too high in the air.

The reptile might have survived if it hadn't lost its temper. It wanted to get to the second tree too quickly, and it moved too suddenly. There was an ominous crack in the greenery, and the creeper again descended by a few feet. The wild boars went totally berserk. They jumped furiously but still in vain.

For the snake, holding onto the liana was quite a challenge. Having reached out its whole length, to proceed further, the serpent had to let go of the trunk of the tree onto which it still held with its tail. It entwined itself around the liana and released its tale in order to keep moving. Just at that moment, a magnificent boar happened to be midair in a prodigious leap. And he made it: he grabbed the end of the serpent's tail. Its massive jaws snapped to and did not let go. The body of the serpent jerked sharply and slipped. Other wild boars caught it with their jaws. And then the massacre began.

They brought the enemy to the ground. The giant would probably have managed two or three, but not two dozen. He bit into the snout of one of the males, but just at that moment, two others sank their fangs into his neck and ripped it apart.

A strong smell of musk filled the air. The pigs, insatiable in their victory, blinded by fury, kept at their terrible task, snapping their jaws and tearing at the flesh. It took them a while to calm down.

Then, several of the animals lifted their heads up as if scenting. Something else suddenly drew their attention. At first, I thought they discovered us. But no, they weren't looking at us at all. Rather, they all turned towards the thicket from which they had come. With signs of fear, they broke up and began to flee through the undergrowth—in a moment, they were all gone, all that is, except the dozen Lasana and I had shot, which lay about dead or dying.

The crash of the vegetation under the trampling hooves of the wild pigs had not yet died down when among the thicket flashed a giant shape: a yellowish, mottled, elongated shape.

"A jaguar!" my heart skipped a beat.

Yes, it was a jaguar following on the heels of the pigs. He, too—it was a male—wanted to take something from the herd for himself. As he crept closer, he stopped in amazement to see so many bodies scattered around: dead and dying pigs.

He was less than thirty paces away. I could see him as plainly as the palm of my hand. I was amazed at how easy it was to understand his reaction: the predator was clearly surprised by the unusual scene.

He crept up quite low, down at the ground, watching the surroundings left and right. You could see he was trying to understand what had happened here.

"He's looking for us!" whispered Lasana.

"Do not move," I whispered under my breath, forgetting in my excitement that I should not speak Arawak.

The jaguar now stared at us and did not divert his gaze. His eyes burned. He had spotted us. Did he think we were edible monkeys?

I will not lie: I shuddered. I had just fired my fowling piece, and there was no time to reload. All I had was my pistol and my old Virginia knife. The pistol was loaded, but whether the powder was dry, I did not know. I carefully felt the handle of the weapon and slowly brought it out in front of me into a firing position. I cocked it.

There was powder in the chamber, and it seemed dry. I sighed with relief.

Meanwhile, the predator did not pay the slightest attention to the wild boars lying on the ground. For some mysterious reason, he was completely focused on us: it seemed to me as if he were devouring us with his eyes. And then it started crawling. Low, crouched, coiled like a spring, with his belly nearly touching the ground, inch by inch, he came closer. There was a hideous menace in this lurking stealth, an inexorable fate from which there was no escape. Our branch was too high for him to reach in a single leap, but I knew he could climb up the trunk of the tree faster than I could even shout for fear.

Holding the pistol with both hands, I aimed it at the animal. At the same time, out of the corner of my eye, I saw that my brave companion had not lost her head, either. She, too, was ready to defend herself. She nocked the last arrow she had left and waited intently for a good moment to shoot. Her calm, her courage, her readiness to fight touched me deeply and filled my heart with a strange tenderness.

The jaguar was still creeping forward. There was no doubt he was going to jump. He crawled to within maybe ten paces and crouched down. His eyes seemed to be sparkling with fire. His utter silence intensified the horror. At last, the beast froze—with the exception of the tail, which swept the ground behind him. Then I saw that the predator raised its rump a little, and I knew it was the last moment before jumping.

I held the pistol before me and aimed squarely at his head. As he tensed to jump, with the tip of my muzzle aligned with his left eye, I pulled the trigger. As my gun blazed, the animal jumped in the air, giving a sharp, short roar. It was a roar—of pain. Having fallen heavily on one side, he lay for a while as if unconscious but then rose with some difficulty and, in a strange, unnatural limp, ran off into the forest. He ran sluggishly, swaying as if drunk, as if something entangled his paws.

"He's hit! He's hit!" cried Lasana. Overcome with joy and relief, she grabbed my arm and pulled me toward herself with strength

I would never have expected from her small body.

"Watch out. We'll fall!" I tried to resist amid the laughter that seized us both as a relief after the superhuman tension.

Gradually, we sobered up and, having calmed down, looked at the battlefield below us with calmer eyes. The jaguar had disappeared in the thicket and ceased to be dangerous: he had probably taken a solid blow to the head. All around us, wild boars lay everywhere, presenting a beautiful and stately scene of a landscape after battle. Fortune had smiled upon us: we had enough meat for our entire tribe for a week. I felt drunk with joy, and my heart seemed about to burst within me. And, as if to complete the perfection of the moment, the glorious sun returned to the sky and dazzled the world all over again, its mighty beams penetrating through the dark forest like golden cords.

Before I got off the tree, I reloaded my fowling piece and my pistol.

Once I reached the ground, I looked up at laughing Lasana and realized suddenly that she had never seemed to me as delicious and as close to my heart as she did at that moment. Laying down my hunting gear by the trunk, I stood under the branch and stretched my arms up to her to help her jump off. She did this gracefully, like a bird of the sky, and fell into my hands like a ripe, delicious fruit. The experience stunned me. All my senses woke within me.

With my left hand, I took her hair roughly at the back of her head and brought her face to mine at arm's length. I looked at her with a gaze that told her everything. I was feasting on every feature of her beautiful face. I drank pleasure from her eyes. Those eyes, hitherto amused, were now watery and misty.

Not letting go of her hair, as if in fear that she might run away, I gathered her at the waist and pulled her to me. She didn't resist. She gripped me tightly in her arms.

We had no time to lie down on the ground before Vagura appeared. He approached joyfully, shouting. We woke up as if from a dream. I released Lasana, she shook out her hair and, touching the back of her head where I had grabbed her, she complained:

"It hurt."

"Did it really hurt?" I asked.

"No," she said.

We finished off the wild boars that were still alive, collected them in one place, and started the tedious work of quartering them. That took the better part of two hours. Then we hung up the meat on branches of trees for our people to collect, tied the two largest animals on a pole, and carried them ourselves, I in front, Vagura in the back. In total had taken over twenty animals, including several shot by Vagura with his blowpipe. We didn't find the Jaguar, but we didn't go looking for him too seriously, either.

Between life and death

As we approached the house, the sun had barely begun to descend from zenith. Boar's meat spoils quickly, so we walked briskly, perhaps too fast. And the accident, which caused my life to hang in the balance, happened not far from our huts, perhaps a hundred paces from the edge of the forest.

Going first, I cradled on my shoulder one end of the branch to which we had died the game. The path was narrow, so narrow that the branches of the bush often slapped us as we walked. I felt just such a slap on my left arm, not too strong or painful, but the sting did not go away. Glancing down, I saw something in the bush nearby. I looked more closely: it was a snake. It was maybe three feet long. It had been sitting on the branch when it bit me. From the shape of its head, I immediately realized that it was a venomous beast.

"Attention!" I said through a constricted throat, as calmly as I could. "I was bitten by a snake!"

"Where?" Vagura jumped up as if woken from sleep.

"Where?"

"On my left arm," I replied, jumping back to the right of the path. "There, you can still see the snake!"

Lasana, who'd been walking behind us, was the closest to the snake. She leaped at it and, using her bow like a stick, with one quick blow, broke the reptile's backbone. It fell off the branch but—did not reach the ground: it hung in the air.

"It's been tied to the branch!" exclaimed Vagura, amazed.

And so it was: the snake had been tied to the branch by its tail. Someone had tied him in our path to make sure it would bite us at a level higher than my boots. And it did.

My companions both jumped on me. I showed them the spot: two tiny spots, difficult to notice if you didn't know what to look for. Utter horror flashed on the faces of my companions.

"Your knife!" commanded Lasana in a voice I had never heard before.

She reached down and tore my knife out of my waistband, but Vagura snatched it from her, saying that he should do it. They told me to sit down.

The boy, gripping me firmly by the arm, cut my flesh where the bite was with three deep, crosswise slashes. Blood gushed from the wound, but he paid it no attention and slashed anew; then he pressed the wound to make it bleed and then slashed again. I ignored the pain, aware of what was at stake.

Then Vigura threw away the knife and, bending down, pressed his mouth to my wound.

"No!" shouted Lasana and pushed him roughly away from me. "You can't!" You have an open cut on your lip!"

She rushed to my arm and started sucking it, spitting blood out every now and then. She not only sucked but chewed scraps of flesh in the wound as if she wanted to bite them off and enlarge the opening. Soon, her whole face, hands, and breasts were blood-stained.

All of this happened lightning-fast, faster than I could possibly describe. No more than a minute had passed from the moment I was bitten when Lasana, panting from the exertion, paused for a moment.

Seeing Vagura standing idly by, she rebuked him sharply and ordered:

"Run to my mother! Tell her what had happened!"

"And?"

"Tell her to get here immediately with the plant she knows."

The boy jumped to it like a deer. My friends clearly loved me.

Sitting as calmly as some minor god, I could not help but be stunned at the sight of their mad excitement and haste. I remembered well the dog that had died so quickly after being bitten, and more than one sad story I had heard about bites of venomous snakes, but feeling no pain other than of the wound Vagura had opened and no discomfort other than light dizziness, I found it hard to understand the extraordinary shock of my friends.

Lasana went back to sucking my wound, but it seemed to bleed less and less, for I must have lost a quart of blood, and clearly we had not cut any larger blood vessels. Seeing the paleness of her face and the constant terror in her eyes, I asked her why she had not let Vagura suck.

"The blood in your wound is poisoned," she explained. "It could poison ten men. If only one drop should enter the veins, one is as good as dead. And Vagura had injured his lip when blowing his blowpipe."

"And you do not have an open wound somewhere? Somewhere you cannot see?"

"I think I do not."

"That's not exactly 'sure,' is it?"

"No one can be sure of anything, ever."

"But you took the risk."

"Yes," she grumbled in a voice which seemed to indicate that she was just doing her duty.

During this brief conversation, I grew more dizzy than before and was seized with sudden anxiety as pain arose in my bitten arm. Suddenly, I began to sweat so violently that whole rivulets began to run off my body. The venom had gotten through and begun its work. The memory of my dog in its death throes stood before my eyes with unbearable clarity.

"You will not die!" I heard Lasana's choked whisper close to my ear, but her voice seemed to reach me as though through a dense fog. "No, you will not die!"

She kept repeating this like a magic spell.

People came running from the settlement, supported my back to make sure I did not lie down, and forced me to drink a disgustingly bitter decoction of some evil herb. My guts were turning over within me with disgust, and I began to vomit terribly as if wishing to empty myself. Repeat convulsions in the stomach—perhaps a dozen in all— exhausted me completely, but at the same time, it seemed as if my head cleared and the pain in my shoulder eased.

Then Arasibo pressed to my lips a huge gourd and poured down my throat exceptionally strong *kashiri*. Others held my head so it wouldn't fall back. Already, after a dozen sips, I was feeling pretty good, but the invalid kept on forcing the stuff down my throat until, completely drunk, I lost consciousness.

When I recovered my senses, it was already dark. I felt numb all over, and my senses revived only partially as if reluctantly returning from another world. Only unbearable thirst kept me awake.

I was lying on my bed in my hut. A fire was burning outside by the entrance, shining in my face. Next to me stood a jug of water on the ground. I reached for it with my right hand and drank greedily. My left arm refused to move.

The sound of drinking alerted my friends, and they all rushed into the hut. When they saw me awake, they rejoiced greatly.

"Your soul has come back to your body!" announced Manauri. "Give him more water to drink!"

I was quite sober but very weak. The pain in my left shoulder had eased, which was taken as a good sign. Arnak touched my forehead.

"He's not sweating anymore," he exclaimed to his friends with visible relief.

It seemed to me, too, that the culmination of the disease had come and gone, and my body had fought off the venom. A terrible venom with terrifying power! Infernal venom of the dragon! After all, that small drop that the snake had pressed just under my skin was almost immediately squeezed or sucked out from the wound, and perhaps only some one-thousandth part of it found its way into my veins. And yet that diluted speck struck down a strong, healthy peasant like myself like a thunderbolt strikes down an aspen tree.

What a great destructive power dwelled in that tiny drop! I shuddered at the thought shuddered and could not comprehend it. Violent evil lurked in this forest. And not just in this forest: it dwelled in this people, too.

"We found two more snakes in the bushes!" announced Arnak.

"Tied?" I asked in a frail voice.

"Tied!"

And he bit his lip.

After a moment, he approached and sat on the ground very close to me. His face was cloudy, his eyes flashed.

"We took counsel together," he said. "What to do. How to end this."

"End what?" I looked at him carefully.

"Some people think it's best to leave Serima and set up our village somewhere, higher up the Imataca. Others insist that no: we stay and we kill Carapana and Coneso. There are more of those in our clan."

Seeing the grimace on my face, he hesitated.

"And what did you decide?"

"To leave Serima is dangerous. The Akawaio are coming. They can come any day, any time. When we are together, we ate strong. If we divide, we will be weak, and they can attack us separately. This means there is no choice but the second option. We kill them. And so we decided. We will go and do it."

Profoundly shocked, I raised myself on my bedding, though I was weak and my bones felt like jelly.

"No!" I called angrily. "No! You must not do it! You must not do it!"

I shouted this repeatedly, as loud as my condition allowed.

Arnak, round-eyed, watched my exultation in utter astonishment. He did not expect such a reaction from a man who had very nearly been murdered.

"Remember! They sent those snakes!" he cried, outraged.

"I remember!"

"And still, you are defending them?"

"I'm not defending them!"

"But you forbid us to kill them!"

"I forbid it!"

Arnak, clearly gripped by fear, studied me as if I had lost my mind. I smiled at him.

"Think carefully, my friend. Think wisely."

"Wisely?" he huffed at me in mockery. "Wisdom says: kill them like the dogs they are! Why don't you let us do it?"

"Look, there are thirty of us. But there are maybe three hundred Arawaks under Coneso."

"Many will come with us."

"Many, but not all. The chief and the sorcerer have great power. You said it yourself more than once. The majority of the people will go with them, and if we kill them, they will try to avenge their deaths. We will end up with the worst possible war: a civil war, a war between brothers. Such wars have destroyed many nations, many of them much greater than the Arawaks. And then there are the Akawaio!"

"Maybe they aren't coming? How do we know?"

"Even if they do not come, it is not a good thing for our tribe to kill each other. Look at it from my point of view. I am sure I am right!"

"Yan! It is about you! We want to protect you!" the boy cried in despair.

Though Arnak's face was usually impassive, yet now, even in the light of the fire outside, I saw what was inside him: a great worry and a great sadness. I put my right hand on his hand in the most sincere gesture I could make and squeezed it tightly.

"I know, Arnak, I know. You are my friend," I nodded my head with great emotion. "But if you're worried about me, then hear me out!"

And in a few words, I laid out my view: because the whole conflict was about me, I didn't want to spill Arawak blood. I was a newcomer here, a guest. Some perhaps thought I was an intruder. It was not reasonable to start a fratricidal war over my person.

Coneso and Carapana were blinded by fear, by a misunderstanding of my objectives. Yes, they were out to destroy me, but I did not lose hope that sooner or later, they would realize their mistake.

"And if they don't? If they kill you first?" interjected Arnak.

"To prevent that, we must redouble our vigilance. Do you understand what I mean?"

"Yes, I do."

I asked the boy to explain my view to Manauri and the others: no hostile steps. It wasn't what they wanted to hear, especially the chief, but they promised to obey me.

It was now already near daybreak, so all the men got up to go to the forest to fetch the slaughtered pigs.

"Lasana and her mother will remain with you," said Arnak before leaving. "They will look after you. Should I give you a weapon to hand?"

"A weapon? I guess give me my pistol. Put it here, where I can easily reach it."

The conversation with my friends exhausted me. After the men left, Lasana came to me and applied a dressing of fresh leaves to my wound.

"Thank you, Charming Palm!" I said.

"What for?"

"For this and for what you did for me in the forest."

"That I drank your blood?" she grinned a broad smile. "It was very tasty! In three days, you will walk again."

"And the wound? When will that heal?"

"That will last longer, maybe much longer. Snake bites do not heal well. You won't be able to use your left arm for some time."

"Then you must be content!"

"Content? Why?" she asked, surprised. "Why would I be content?"

"Because it will not be able to pull your hair again!"

"Ah!" she bent low over me with a flicker in her eyes. "You do have another hand, you know."

But then she took a step away from me, suddenly deeply troubled, and stared at me searchingly as if she wanted to see through me.

"Hey, you!" I chuckled, amused. "Don't you recognize me?"

"No!" she replied firmly.

"This is me, White Jaguar!" I went on with the joke.

"I noticed something there, in the forest," she said slowly and thoughtfully as if to herself. "You speak our language! How is this possible?"

"I learned."

"When?"

"I have heard all of you speak: Arnak, Vagura, Manauri, you. Especially you!"

I chuckled again.

"What is so funny?"

"I just remembered a late-night conversation between a certain beautiful palm and her chief. Near Mount Vulture. On the ship."

"Oh, yes?"

"Yes!"

"And you understood it?"

"Yes."

"And you said nothing?"

"You two were talking... I didn't want to interrupt you."

I guessed from her eyes how embarrassed she was, how confused, how abashed. She was lost for words.

"You have nothing to be ashamed of!" I stroked her hand tenderly. "Manauri wanted you to possess me, to manipulate me. But you, out of your uncommon dignity—refused. How nobly you put up resistance! How brave and forthright you were. I was very proud of you. I began to admire you. "

"So I did possess you, after all!" she snorted.

"Ha! I guess... I guess you have," I admitted. "And do you want to own me even more completely?"

She was silent for a while. Then said simply:

"I do."

"Then tell no one that I can speak Arawak. Let this remain our secret."

And somehow, about then, a great weariness came over me; my eyelids became heavy, and tired thoughts became confused in my mind. Lasana spoke more, but I couldn't hear it; I was falling asleep or perhaps unconscious.

I was tormented by nightmares: fratricidal battles, monstrous snakes, and stubborn, vicious, screaming quarrels. Finally, a noisome jabbering pierced the shell of my sleep, and I began to wake up. The sounds of arguing came from outside—and it was a real fight. I sobered up in the blink of an eye, recognizing the voices of those who were arguing: Lasana against Coneso and Carapana. Lasana would not allow them to enter my hut.

"No, you can't," she snarled, seething, angry and firm. "Manauri forbade it!"

"He forbade me to enter? Me, the chief?"

"Everyone! You, too!"

"I think you should step aside, you nagging witch, or I'll smash your head in! We just want to see him. See him and help him!"

Lasana concluded that, in a straight-up fight, she could not beat two men, and everyone else was still in the forest.

"Very well," she agreed after some hesitation. "But you must leave your weapons outside. I will not let you in with your maces!"

"Fine, we will do as you wish, you shrew," said Coneso.

"A female dog," growled the sorcerer under his breath.

It was already broad daylight, the sun had risen maybe an hour ago. In the hut, it was still twilight as the entrance was hung with a deer skin. As soon as I had heard the voices, I reached for my pistol and cocked it, then held it in my right hand under the mat under which I was resting. I placed the pistol along my right thigh, holding it by the handle, my finger on the trigger.

The two men slipped in, and behind them—Lasana. They left the entrance uncovered, letting in more light. They approached my bed.

Lasana stopped on the other side, watching their every movement.

I was lying on my back, my head upraised a little on a pillow of grass. I kept my eyes half closed and motionless, staring into the ceiling somewhere above the entrance, as unconscious people sometimes do. I could just make out their figures with my peripheral vision.

They stared down at me for a long time, saying nothing. Then Carapana lowered his head to the level of my eyes and studied me carefully. He stared long, long, so long that I began to worry that I might betray myself with a reckless move. I saw his Adam's apple move up and down.

"The poison has done a pretty thorough job," he said at last, making a grimace as if to giggle. "He's half dead already."

"Will he die?" asked Coneso.

"I think he will."

"When?"

I don't know. Maybe soon."

They spoke to each other in front of Lasana without any embarrassment and convinced that I did not understand them. But I heard and understood every word they said.

"His eyes are half open," observed the chief suspiciously.

"But they don't see much," Carapana reassured him. "Unless..."

"Unless?"

"Unless he is pretending."

Now it was Coneso's turn to bring his face right up to mine and stare at me intently.

"He looks pale. But he still breathes."

"He won't breathe long!" growled the sorcerer, and once again, his wrinkled, malignant face loomed before me. He fixed me with a look so terrible and hateful that I no longer had any doubt which one of them wanted me dead.

"And if he is pretending?" asked Coneso.

"Even so, he won't live long," repeated Carapana, self-confident in his stubbornness.

Until then, I had followed everything that was going on around me with equanimity, feeling reassured by the pistol in my hand. But when I heard the sorcerer's last words, containing a mysterious threat, I somehow felt uneasy, and my heart leaped at a gallop. Where was the danger coming from?

"Lasana!" the sorcerer turned to the woman. "Show us his wound."

"We will not touch it," said the chief. "To make sure no one suspects us."

"It is wrapped with leaves," objected Lasana.

"Did you bandage him?"

"No, my mother did."

"Summon your mother, then."

Lasana hesitated whether to leave us alone but, after a while, decided that she could risk it: she did not have far to go: she stepped out before the entrance and shouted for her mother, who lived less than a quarter mile away. In a few words, she asked her to come, and she returned inside the hut.

A Dancing Caribbean Woman
Christoph Weigel after Caspar Luyken
Neu-eröffnete Welt-Galleria, Nürnberg 1703

While she was out—and it lasted only a few moments—something mysterious happened at my bedside. Carapana dashed behind my back, leaning forward a little, but what he did there, I did not know, for I did not dare turn my head. A faint, curious murmur reached my ears. It was hard to guess its source. Was it a slight bubbling or buzzing, maybe rustling? Besides, there was too little time left for reflection, for Lasana had already rushed back in and inspected everything with a distrustful eye, both the hut and the two men. Apparently, she did not notice anything suspicious because she calmly announced that her mother would arrive shortly.

When the woman arrived, she uncovered my wound, luckily without lifting the mat from my right side where the pistol was. Carapana praised the dressing and gave the women his own herbs, which he considered more effective for wound closure. But then he added that it was not certain that they would work because it seemed to him nothing could save the patient.

"Nothing can save him?" the old woman was surprised. "He is already better!"

"I see no improvement," announced the sorcerer severely. "How long has he been this stiff?"

"For some time now, but earlier, he'd been moving."

"He's gone numb because of the approaching death. He will die by nightfall."

The woman was of a different opinion, but she did not dare to contradict Carapana and the definitive announcement he had made.

"He will die," repeated the sorcerer, clearly enjoying himself. "He will die because he was bitten by an unusual snake."

"Unusual?"

"Yes, unusual. Enchanted."

"Oh, we know very well who enchanted the snake and tied it to the bush!" snorted Lasana angrily.

"You silly, arrogant girl!" the sorcerer chided her with grim seriousness. "You could never guess who bewitched the snake!"

"Oh, yes? Who, then?"

"He did!"

"He? White Jaguar?"

"Yes!"

There fell an eloquent silence, indicating clearly that the women did not believe the sorcerer's words.

"Yes, he did!" Carapana reassured them. "You, Lasana, are young and naive, but your mother can tell you that there are all kinds of *kanaima*. And the worst are those who impersonate good people. Why, a person can be a good person and not know that he has an evil, burning, pernicious soul. While his body sleeps, the soul detaches itself from him and does terrible things, harms people and animals, kills, sucks blood, poisons, sends venomous snakes. Are there such people? Tell me!" he asked the old woman.

"Yes, there are," admitted the old woman, intimidated.

"And what do you, silly girl, know about him, your White Jaguar? Do you know his inhuman crimes, committed in his sleep, when perhaps he himself does not know what he is doing? When perhaps he himself does not know his own soul, his *kanaima* nature?"

"And how do you recognize such a soul?" asked Lasana.

"Look at my face, girl, and see how old I am. That's how many years of experience I have. Can you see my face? Do you have eyes?"

"I do have eyes, and I can see," she replied hardily. "And I see no *kanaima* in him, but in you, I see anger and hatred, even though you are a great sorcerer!"

There was a moment of silence. I decided that if the sorcerer were to strike Lasana, I would shoot him in the head. But he didn't strike her. He smothered his fury. He just said calmly, in a hoarse voice:

"This *kanaima* will die tonight. And you, you vicious shrew, you be careful that you do not die with him."

He said this and appeared to prepare to leave. Then Coneso rushed to Lasana and, seizing her arms with both hands, began to shake her furiously.

"If you understand what Carapana says and want to live," he

salivated with lust and anger at once, 'if you want to live, you know what to do! There is only one way to save yourself from death. You must go to my hut. Today. Tonight."

"Do not touch me!" I heard her cold answer. "I will never go to your hut."

"Lasana, Lasana!" Coneso suddenly spoke with a plea in his voice. "I want you to live! Please leave this place and come to me. You will live! You will live!"

Then, suddenly, he let go and followed Carapana outside. The Sorcerer was already disappearing among the huts.

After they left, the women quickly calmed down. The mother asked the daughter, pointing at me:

"Did they touch him?"

"No."

This calmed the old woman but did not dispel her bitterness. She watched me reluctantly, without warmth. Had the sorcerer's ridiculous ravings about my allegedly harmful soul made an impression on her after all? Or perhaps she resented the trouble I had inadvertently caused them?

I smiled at her, but she didn't respond. Only when I took the gun out from under the mat, the women chuckled in relief, pleased to know that they had not been entirely defenseless before Coneso and Carapana. By that small revelation, I seemed to steel back into the old woman's graces.

The women immediately set about examining the herbs offered by Carapana to see if he had mixed anything poisonous while I carefully examined the place by the bed where the sorcerer performed his mysterious gurgling. There, on the ground, I saw a jug with drinking water for me—the jug and nothing else. Suddenly, it dawned on me. I understood everything, and I felt a hot wave wash over my body. There was no doubt: the strange soft gurgling I had heard was the sound of the water in the jug. Carapana had put something in my jug! Poison? Poison, of course! That was why the sorcerer was so sure that I would die that night. Were it not for my vigilance, I would not have discovered his cunning design until too late.

"Take heart!" I called. "I have a surprise for you!"

I ordered Lasana to fetch an old gourd, pour water from my jug into it, and give it to drink to a dog that had come to our hut with the two guests and was still roaming nearby.

"That's Coneso's dog," observed Lasana's mother.

"All the better."

I wasn't sure whether my suspicions would prove correct. The dog lapped up the water contentedly, then pranced in front of the hut with other mutts. But after a quarter of an hour, Lasana ran in with a message. Coneso's best friend fell down like struck by lightning and was flailing its paws in a death trance. It had succumbed to poison.

I smiled ear to ear with contentment when Lasana reported this to me, but at the bottom of my heart, I felt a deep sense of anxiety. The fierce hate of the sorcerer filled me with unwitting terror.

And with a strong resolution that there was no choice after all and that I would have to fight Carapana, I fell asleep again.

I was woken by loud voices. This time, happy ones. The men had returned from the forest with the game. They deposited the carcasses in front of my hut: there was a whole pile of meat. Arnak and Vagura rushed in. They were carrying a jaguar skin stretched on bamboo poles.

"There it is!" yelled Vagura. "He's dead!"

"The whole skin! Undamaged, unpunctured, uncut!" exalted Arnak. "No holes anywhere! Did you kill him by magic?"

My friend was, of course, joking. He knew perfectly well how I killed the cat, but his joke gave me an idea.

"Maybe by magic!" I said, smiling. "Magic is not a stupid thing. I should use it more often. How far did he manage to escape?"

"A hundred paces. You shot him in the left eye, right into the brain."

Now, others came in: Manauri, Miguel, and other Indians, all of whom I now knew by name, all in high spirits.

"Ten and ten, and eight," they counted.

"So many wild pigs!" rejoiced Manauri. "How shall we divide them? You shot them, you decide."

"Very well. We give twelve to the people of Coneso," I said. "Eight to the people of Pirokai, and the other eight remain for us."

"Isn't that a little too much for them?" Manauri expressed his doubts.

"No. There are many more of them than of us."

"And Carapana? Will he get nothing?"

"Oh, yes, he will. He will get—the jaguar skin."

"The jaguar skin? The jaguar skin?"

They all thought I had misunderstood Manauri's question. Give the murderer and poisoner Carapana the jaguar skin?

"Yes, you heard me well. Carapana will get the jaguar skin!"

Vagura put his hands to his head in an expression of shock, and others began to shout past each other:

"Don't do such a thing! Such a beautiful skin to that scoundrel? This is madness! It is your emblem. Why give it to him?"

"Yes, we give it to him!" I said, amused by their stunned faces.

"Yan! Yan!" objected Arnak. "He will misunderstand you. He will think that you are afraid of him and trying to buy him off."

"I insist. He will get the skin. And I assure you he will understand me well!"

After that, the two women told my friends how the sorcerer had come to poison me.

The Jaguar Eye

The Arawak nation, whose northern branch now lived on the Imataca, undoubtedly enjoyed a better quality of life than most of the South

American tribes, especially the woodlanders. It was an agricultural tribe, unlike the Akawaio or most other Carib tribes; agricultural, meaning that it derived most of its sustenance from the cultivation of land. This required them to adopt a sedentary mode of life, and that, in turn, allowed them the opportunity to develop certain crafts. And thus, the Arawaks, or rather their women, were famous for their pottery and their weaving. Multicolored fabrics woven on simple lap looms, as well as ingenious pots, sometimes of enormous size, were highly sought after by other Indians as objects of trade. Whenever it wasn't raining, Lasana's mother spent several hours each day sitting outside weaving intricately patterned mats out of vegetable fibers.

Still, even if the Arawaks enjoyed greater comfort and prosperity than other tribes, they were just as ensnared by a web of superstition as all their neighbors were. They were plagued by magic spells, curses, ghosts, and demons. Sometimes, it seemed to me as if their dark beliefs imitated the terribly confusing forest that surrounded them on all sides: they were just as tangled, dark, confused, and difficult to break through as the surrounding jungle.

Demons, usually malicious and always restless, could take various forms: now of some terrible animal, now of monstrous bogeymen, or become invisible and thereby even more dangerous. They tormented people in their dreams by poisoning their blood, they confused hunters' paths and minds in the forest, they brought diseases, and caused sudden death. The common man was practically defenseless against them, though he shielded himself with amulets as much as he could. And yet, there were also those among them who maintained an impure covenant with the forces of evil or even transformed themselves into demons or into bloodthirsty beasts at will.

Such terrible ghost-people did their neighbors much harm, and the sorcerer of a tribe had to exert all his powers to detect them and put them to death. Particular fear was aroused by a kind of evil creature who, as a person, could be innocent, kind, and full of goodness but, without knowing it, possessed the bloodthirsty soul of a demon. When he or she slept, their soul stealthily left their body and wandered around doing terrible mischief, even to their own families. These involuntary enemies of the tribe were the hardest to track down and eradicate. Carapana's rascally suggestion that I had just such a perverse soul could have caused quite a lot of trouble for me because how could I possibly clear myself of such an accusation?

Perhaps because they had been away from the jungle and had seen a bit of the world, our people were not quite so enthralled by superstition as their brethren. And Arnak seemed completely inured to it.

On the following day, I asked Arnak, Vagura, Manauri, Arasibo, and Lasana to come to my bedside because I wanted to present to them a plan of action against the sorcerer.

"At last!" growled Manauri. "You've finally seen the light! How do we kill him?"

"Oh, no! We must not kill him!"

"Then he will continue to harass us!"

"We will fight him with the weapon he is using against us: magic."

"Magic?" the chief stretched out the word doubtfully. And then I explained to them what I had planned.

"You, Arnak, and two of your friends will take the skin of the jaguar to Carapana and solemnly declare to him that it is a gift from me. Say that the eye through which I killed the beast has a bewitching power and sees everything the sorcerer is up to and immediately reports it to the Jaguar's skull, and the skull remains with me to reveal everything to me in turn. This is how it revealed to me the poison that had been put in my drinking water and why Coneso's dog had to die. You will say that removing the skin or destroying it will not help Carapana, for the magic eye, all-seeing as it is, will inform the skull and me anyway. You will also say that my jaguar skin shields me from all dangers and turns every attack on me against the perpetrator. Just like the dog of Coneso, every man who attacks me will perish. Tell him that until now, I have been patient and forgiving, but that, starting today, fun and games are over, and I will no longer tolerate any more attacks on me and my people. Can you do that?"

"Yes. I will!"

"And you think this will tame Carapana?" Manauri hung his lower lip doubtfully.

"I think, yes," I replied, though I wasn't really sure.

The method seemed naive, but I was counting on the morbid imagination and superstitious perversity of Carapana and his henchmen.

"Oh, yes!" exclaimed Arasibo in a sudden outburst of ferocious zeal. "This will tame him! He will be afraid. The Jaguar's eye will bewitch him!"

Manauri glanced at him askance.

"And you, why do you yell like that?" he barked. "You fool!"

"Arasibo is not so stupid!" Arnak came to the invalid's defense and added cheerfully: "Arasibo is half-sorcerer himself. He knows all of Carapana's tricks!"

The chief shrugged, but Arasibo exclaimed forcefully:

"Carapana will be afraid of the eye, I tell you. He will be afraid of the eye of the jaguar!"

The skin, already treated against parasites with a decoction of a poisonous liana, could be sent ahead without fear of decay. My legation found Carapana in his ceremonial hut, which stood apart from all others, a few hundred paces from the rest of the Coneso settlement. The sorcerer greeted Arnak with a sneer, and when he heard my message, he showed no fear or embarrassment but rather seemed glad to receive such beautiful skin.

"Remember: the left eye is enchanted!" Arnak repeated to him with menacing emphasis as if Carapana had not heard his words. The left eye obeys White Jaguar and reports everything to him."

"Because White Jaguar shot the left eye?" asked the sorcerer.

"Yes."

"But he didn't damage the right eye?"

"No."

"He didn't, you say?"

Carapana croaked an inhuman laugh that sounded like barking and turned into a protracted howl so eery that Arnak and his two companions shuddered.

"He did not damage the right eye?" croaked the sorcerer. "So only this left eye obeys White Jaguar! And the right—does it obey him or not? Speak!"

"I don't know," stammered the youth.

"White Jaguar said nothing about the right eye? Speak!"

"No, nothing."

"Ha! He didn't tell you, did he?" boomed the old man. "Well then, I will tell you! Do you know to whom the right eye of the beast will obey?"

"Eh?"

"Why, the left eye obeys the White Jaguar, but the right eye... obeys me!"

And he kept up his unstoppable laughter as if he were chanting an evil spell; as if he wasn't laughing but beating the men on their heads with his laughter like a club:

"Obeys me! Obeys me!"

Half an hour later, in my hut, we were listening to Arnak's report, and our hearts sank.

"I told you right away!" Manauri pointed out. "Carapana is a great sorcerer, undefeated, invincible. He laughed at you. He mocked your magic! You can't stifle him with a tale. There is only one way to deal with him!"

"I know, I know!" I hissed impatiently. "A bullet in the head."

"Exactly: a bullet in the head!"

"No!" I said firmly. "No way."

"He laughed at your magic!" the chief tormented me. "'The jaguar's right eye obeys him.' Him! We didn't think about the right eye..."

But Arasibo interrupted him impatiently. His anger and his ardor were emphasized by the scowl of his face and the way he screwed up his crossed eyes.

"Not true!" he gagged. "The right eye of the jaguar will not obey him!"

"Phew!" he snorted Manauri mockingly. "It will not obey him? You will prevent it? You are so strong?"

"I! Yes, I!" Arasibo announced as if hitting a stump with an axe.

We all looked at the invalid, so strangely excited.

Feverish fires burned in his pupils. In a choked voice, in a whisper breathless with excitement, he told us what was on his mind: White Jaguar can sleep peacefully and can recover safely. Carapana will not reach him. Carapana is a great sorcerer and very evil, but he will have no power over the beast's right eye. The beast's skull is in our hands. Only through the skull can the eyes exercise their magical power. He, Arasibo, will seal the right socket of the skull, and the eye will see nothing. Nothing. And therefore, Carapana will see nothing. And Arasibo will set up the jaguar skull outside my hut so that everyone can see that the right eye is blind."

"And what if they steal the skull?" Manauri winced, then contemptuously snorted through his nose.

"Let them try!" the cross-eye burned with hate. "Let them try! Day and at night, I will watch the skull! I will sooner die than let anyone take it!"

My friends fell silent, deep in thought, pondering Arasibo's words. At that moment, a strange impotence seized me. My head spun, frightened thoughts refused to obey me. I felt sick. I felt nauseous, nauseous, and short of breath. Perhaps it was a result of the snake venom, but I suddenly felt cruelly lonely with my sorrows. Who were these people who surrounded me? Were they really my friends? In the deep shadows, their brown faces became dark, almost invisible, and that made me suffer more. Behold, a violent fear of the strangeness of these people and their world grabbed me by the throat and choked me. I was afraid that they and I would never understand each other properly.

How did this happen? I invented that business with the jaguar's enchanted eye. I invented it only semi-seriously, almost as a frolic, to scare a dangerous madman, drive him into a corner, force him to come to his senses, act rationally, come to terms. After all, such a ridiculous idea as a jaguar's eye could only have arisen as a joke—in my mind, in my friends's minds, how else! But the joke, bouncing off Carapana's head like a billiard ball, returned to us in—and in what a changed form! The joke ceased to be a joke, the jaguar's eye and his skin and his skull took on the reality of powerful magic, and our lame Arasibo, an honest and devoted simpleton, now went into raptures, talking with extraordinary seriousness about casting spells, countering magic with magic, and making of me a great shaman. And my friends accepted this for good coin and pondered what he said?

I felt short of breath. An unknown fear came over me. Everything here, imbued with spells, ghosts, and monsters, became hostile, inhuman, incomprehensible. It breathed the terror of strangeness. From the darkness of the forest and from the darkness of these superstitious souls, demons broke into my mind. Demons and superstitions became a hostile barrier between me and my closest allies. They took away kind, human, relatable qualities from them. Something howled in me with a morbid longing: I longed for *man*. An honest, friendly, warm being who laughed off the idiocy of a *jaguar's eye*.

I was finding it difficult to breathe. Nausea engulfed me. I felt hideous pressure in the head and pain, sharp pain. The world darkened before my eyes. Then I heard Arnak's frightened voice as if from a great distance.

"Yan! Yan! What is going on with you? Look how he sweats! He's fainting!"

His voice, his dear voice, full of concern, of love, seemed to comfort my fainting heart. It seemed to give me strength. I felt my senses returning to me. I forced a smile and looked around.

"Who's fainting?" I asked.

"I thought that you..." he murmured in English.

How grateful I was to him for speaking to me in my language.

He touched my forehead tenderly; at the same time, I felt a strong, tender pressure in my palm: Lasana held me by the hand. And suddenly, I was myself again, my weakness gone.

All were still the way they had been a moment ago, Manauri scowling, taunting, fierce, Arasibo profoundly moved, with sparkling eyes.

"Carapana? He mocked our message!" the chief stubbornly repeated himself. "He mocked us, he mocked our jaguar! He laughed in your face! He laughed! Haha!"

Suddenly, his voice changed:

"Bullet to the head, I say."

Arasibo waved his hands in the direction of Manauri to break the torrent of his virulence and then turned to Arnak, himself uncommonly affected:

"I know him through and through! I know him like the devil!"

"I believe it," mumbled the youth, surprised by his virulence.

"Tell me, Arnak, tell me! How did he look when he received you? How did he look when he laughed?"

"How did he look? Normal, I suppose. Except that he laughed."

"And what about his Adam's apple? Did it move up and down? Do you remember?"

"Yes, it did."

"Really quickly? Up and down? Like a rat in a cage?"

"Heh, when you put it like this, yes, it was rather like a rat in a cage."

"Up and down? Real quick? You're sure?"

"Yes."

Arasibo slowly turned to Manauri, his face crooked in anger and contempt:

"Do you hear?"

"I hear it," snorted the chief. "What of it?"

"This, chief: Carapana laughed with his mouth, but in his

heart, he had fear. I know that scum! When his Adam's apple goes up and down, it's a sign. He is worried. He is afraid."

The invalid's words made a strong impression on everyone. Only Manauri gave him no credence and held his own:

"But he sneered! Sneered!"

"He was scared!" shouted Arasibo.

"He laughed!" the chief spoke yet louder.

"He laughed, but he trembled inside!"

They stood facing each other enraged, both in an ineffable, unintelligent state of fury. They devoured each other with their eyes, full of stubbornness.

Again, nausea engulfed me. I felt weak. I felt revulsion. Blood rushed to my head. The world grew dark again.

"Enough!" I groaned with the last of my strength. "People! Think rationally!"

They looked at me, confused and embarrassed. They restrained their anger, they softened, their faces smoothed.

"Let's go away," whispered Arnak. "Let's let him sleep."

They left.

Only Lasana remained by my side. She came to my bedside, knelt down, leaned in. I saw concern and great attachment in her good, damp eyes. Her eyes seemed to me even more than beautiful: they were maternal. She was kind. She was giving and devoted to me. But was she close? Did she understand what terrified me? Did she realize how tormented I felt by my Arawaks' strangeness, by their hostile, superstitious world?

"I can't breathe," I sighed.

She inclined still closer. She looked into my eyes. Her hair fell over my face. Contradictory scents mixed in it: the smell of a woman's warmth and the odor of the wild forest. Lasana must have noticed the alarming grimace on my face. It worried her.

"What suffocates you?" she asked softly.

"Their hate."

"Whose? Carapana's?"

"Not just Carapana's. Manauri's, Arasibo's."

She wondered. She hesitated for a moment. She dove deep into herself, into her thoughts, looking for understanding.

"I do not hate," she said at last, slowly, clearly, stressing her words.

"Their anger, their hostility poisons me!" I complained witlessly.

"Oh, Yan... I am not hateful. I do not hate."

"Ah, Lasana! Do you understand me? Their darkness overwhelms me. Their belief in magic sucks me into a great darkness."

"But I am like the sunlight. There is no darkness in me."

"Oh, dear girl! You belong to them!"

"No, Yan! No! I belong... to you."

Her voice breathed great tenderness. She did not allow herself to be pushed away. She fought for a place by my side. Her eyes were wide open. Our eyes locked as if in an embrace. Blood flowed through our hearts with a stronger pulse. I reached out with my right hand and touched her shoulder. It felt as if I touched life itself. A warm current passed from her to me.

The following morning, after sleeping for many hours, I woke up significantly healthier and stronger. I got up and, after several minutes, went outside. The gloom of the previous day had dissipated, and a new spirit had entered into me.

On a stake, a man and a half high, driven into the ground twenty-odd paces from my hut, sat the skull of the jaguar. The ants had cleaned it of all flesh, and now it shone from a distance, its large teeth gleaming with a predatory smile. The left eye socket—"mine"— glared black with an open cavity, while the right one, plastered over with clay and wood shavings, was blind and from a distance— invisible. You would think that the thing sitting there was only our totem, our family crest, and yet we have imbued it with the terrible power to break and destroy our enemy.

Looking at Arasibo's handiwork, I shuddered despite myself.

The invalid sat nearby, watching, and as soon as he saw me, he came out of his hiding, limping. His ugly mouth smiled ear to ear.

"You see, how nice it looks?" he greeted me joyfully. "I never let my eye off it!"

The skull turned its lone eye socket in the direction of Serima and the hut of Carapana. Between that village and us grew a stretch of the jungle, a narrow strip left uncleared and reaching all the way down to the water, so Serima and Carapana's hut were invisible. But the skull bared its fangs in that direction.

Arasibo was in exceptionally good humor.

"What makes you so happy?" I asked him.

"I'm happy! Oh, I am happy!" he replied with a mysterious expression but not hiding his pride. He pointed to the skull with his thumb: "The seed has sprouted!"

"What seed?"

"Carapana is going crazy! Don't you hear the *maraca*?"

Several friends emerged out of their huts and approached us. They were extremely excited, and they confirmed Arasibo's words: the sorcerer had gone mad. As soon as Arasibo had put up the skull on the preceding day, Carapana learned about it from his spies and started a series of magical rituals to counteract the Evil Eye. He'd gone mad, they said. Like a madman, he started dancing around his ceremonial hut and was still dancing without having slept a wink at night. The horrible screams of his incantations sent him into foaming, trembling spasms.

Indeed, I could hear the sound of odd rattling coming from Serima and the beating of a magic drum. The people in Serima were seized with great fear.

"What is this *maraca*?"

"The sorcerer's most important tool!"

It turned out to be an empty shell of a hard fruit with pebbles inside: a simple rattle, but with immeasurable magical power.

"And it's not going to help him!" Arasibo giggled, and his

whole face beamed with cruelty, hatred, and insane contentment.

"We got him, White Jaguars. We got him! And we will not let go!"

"Is it up to us?" I asked doubtfully

"It's up to the Eye!" Arasibo croaked triumphantly. "It's all in the the Eye!"

"Maybe he can break it?"

"He cannot! He will dance until he falls down with exhaustion, senseless! He will lie down like a dying dog, then he will get up, he will thrash again, he will faint again, and this will go on and on and on until the end!"

"Will he die?"

"Yes! He will die! He will lose his mind, his heart will break, he will die!" Arasibo, full of vengeance for wrongs he had suffered, was gloating in unhealthy delight. But other people in our clan did not share in his enthusiasm. They were terrified of Carapana's powers, and they feared that even if the sorcerer died, his monstrous madness might cause him to haunt us and commit malicious crimes. A rabid dog is dangerous. How much more dangerous is a rabid sorcerer! They were afraid. They did not triumph.

But Arasibo went on:

"We got him!" he gnashed his teeth. "The skull will kill him!"

Lasana's mother noticed me in the yard, she came running, growled furiously, and ordered me to bed.

After many hours of rest, I couldn't take it anymore and got up again. It was evening.

"You are so strong!" Lasana poked fun at me, clearly pleased with my progress. "You are a true Jaguar! You overcame the serpent's venom!"

"I owe it to you, Charming Palm!"

"You are so strong! So full of life!" she looked me over, head to foot, with clear pleasure.

We were laughing, happy. I recovered quickly. From afar, from beyond the forest, from the direction of Serima, the incessant, dull rumble of a drum kept coming. The three of us, Arnak, Arasibo, and I, went out to take a look. We went slowly, gingerly. We had brought our guns and the spyglass.

Having passed the wood that separated us from Serima, we stopped on the edge of the thicket, hidden from the eyes of the villagers. Carapana's cottage stood a little out of the way, at the edge of the jungle, to our right. From a distance of about three hundred paces, we could see it clearly because a stretch of cleared land stretched all around the village.

We saw him right away. He was running around his hut dancing. Staggering, actually, as if drunk. He hooted wild spells, he summoned vengeful spirits, and in his mental confusion, he stamped his feet and flailed his arms. In each hand, he shook a *maraca*, and their rattling echoed through the forest and over the river. His apprentice sat on the ground next to him. He was beating the drum.

Ha! Carapana fell for it big time. He'd been dancing and raging the whole day and the whole night. He didn't look tired, he must have taken some strength-enhancing herb.

He hurled hideous curses, but it was obvious that he was alone, enslaved by a more powerful curse, caught up in an invisible noose. He struggled like a beast of prey on a chain. Will he break the bond?

"He will die," Arasibo gurgled oddly with delight. "He's losing his mind!"

The sight was shocking and revolting and, at the same time, satisfying: here was fate delivering justice. Before our eyes unfolded some mysterious, hideous business, but whatever we thought about it, we were sure of one thing: Carapana had fallen in a snare from which he would probably be unable to free himself. He would not escape its destiny.

"People say that if he loses his mind, he can become *kanaima* and harm us," I observed.

"Maybe this is so," confirmed Arnak.

"No!" objected Arasibo testily. "He will die first!"

Excitement did not dull the invalid's vigilance. His mind was alert, his eyes open. Understanding well the pernicious influence of the jaguar skull on the sorcerer, he had watched it like the apple of his eye, and at night, he hid it in a hiding place known only to himself.

Meanwhile, Carapana did not follow the inevitable road to perdition, as Arasibo had imagined and we had begun to believe. Perhaps the sorcerer had mastered his madness. He no longer wandered madly around the hut, and soon, the dry rattling of the *maracas* stopped, and only the drum still growled. But it was not a sorcerer who beat it, but his young apprentice.

"He's gone inside to lie down. He is dying," Arasibo reassured us.

The Sickness of the Child

He didn't die. People saw him in the village. Talked to him. He was said to have terrible eyes, like those of an unconscious beast. He sowed fear and respect even greater than before. And he did not intend to give up or compromise. In those satanic days, he hatched an idea in his cunning head. From Serima, a new, great danger blew towards me.

Lasana's child, the nearly one-and-a-half-year-old son of the African hero Mateo, who had died on Robinson's Island, was struck by a mysterious disease. The boy began to run a fever, his body covered with sores, he cried in pain and lost weight. The ministrations of Lasana's mother, whose medications had brought me so quickly back to health, proved in vain. No herbs, no ointments, no treatments helped. The child withered day by day. And from the first hours of his sickness, there appeared, no one knew whence, disturbing rumors, at first incomprehensible and airy like the lightest breeze, then more and more persistent like flies, then insistent like poisonous fumes:

rumors about my harmful soul. People—not only people from Serima but also people of our clan began to whisper. I saw their skittish glances and fast-averted eyes. As the child's illness progressed, the bad talk grew thicker and already unambiguously linked me with the misfortune: my perverse soul was killing the child. Lasana loved him very much and was distraught when the mother's medicines had no effect.

She came to my hut and stood above me upright, with a serious and resolute expression, her eyes glazed over with sorrow, and she said cordially and courageously, with great solemnity:

"Do not listen to what people say! I am with you!" she reassured me.

My four best friends said the same thing to me, with a vertical crease of concern on their foreheads: Arnak, Vagura, Manauri, and Miguel. They assured me that the hostile gossip would soon pass, that it would turn away from me and perish. But I often saw them deep in unhappy thoughts or watching with attentive eyes the nearby huts and the edge of the forest. Only Arasibo remained gloomily silent, but he, too, was looking around suspiciously, crouching, waiting.

On the third or fourth day of the child's illness, things came to a boil among the Arawaks on the Imataca. Carapana, by virtue of his office in the tribe, declared to all and sundry that invisible powers revealed to him who was to blame for the child's illness. Blame the White Jaguar. In a dream, the spirits showed the sorcerer this picture: many weeks ago, during a rapid march across the steppe to the north, White Jaguar snatched the child from Lasana's hands and held it to his chest, carrying it for a long time. During that embrace, his soul possessed the child's soul and meted out death to him. If the child dies now—and it will die for sure!—it will be clear who is responsible for his death.

"Yes, he did!" Vagura raised his hands to his face in shock. "Yan took Lasana's baby in his arms to help her carry it! I remember! We all remember!"

Arnak glared at him indignantly.

"Carapana learned about this by chance from someone, for it was never a secret. In fact, we all talked about it then. So he heard the story, and now he has twisted everything against Yan. We should have shot the monster like Manauri said."

This was not a child's play. Suddenly, an imminent danger hung over me, an abyss opened before my feet, everything hung by a hair. Voices were heard in Coneso's circle to drive me out of the tribe before I caused the death of others. Others recommended that I be killed. But the sorcerer alone—gracious and considerate—opposed them. Let us wait to see, he said, if he kills the child; and if he does, then kill him! So he counseled the exasperated people of Serima, and a word of these conversations reached our settlement quickly.

"The kid will probably die," said Manauri gloomily.

The chief was very distressed by the situation as if feeling guilty that he had brought me to the village, that he had exposed me to danger. But he had not brought me here. I had wanted to come with my friends. I had come of my own volition. Manauri knew also that if I was killed by Carapana's men, he would be killed next. This knowledge filled him with apprehension, and I could see the superhuman effort with which he tried to keep himself in check, to keep up steady, calm appearances.

In those hard days, I got to know my friends. Arnak never wavered for a moment, nor did he lose his head. He was ready to die in my defense. Vagura remained steadfastly by me, though I could see that the talk about me carrying the child had shaken him. The five Africans, led by Miguel, came to me and declared they would see the conflict to the end at my side.

In fact, most of the men of our clan have found a way to reassure me that they would not abandon me despite the various ties that connected them with family and friends in Serima. And Pedro— what choice did he have?—his fate was bound with mine. We would live or die together.

In all this time of great tension, Arasibo caused me deep anxiety. He acted strangely, very strangely. He became gloomy, silent, squinted at everyone suspiciously from under a lowered head, like a bull prepared for a fight. He remained stubbornly silent as if he had lost his tongue, he spoke to no one, but he did not shun us; on the contrary, he clung to us. Whenever we assembled in my hut to talk, he always sat at the entrance and looked stubbornly at the yard and pricked up his ears so as not to miss a word. When approached, he muttered indistinctly and repulsively: his eyes looked mean and evil. Arnak and Vagura regarded him more and more distrustfully.

Though the clan stood by me, there was no more talk about fighting or killing Carapana. More and more often, there was talk of moving away, somewhere up the Imataca. We had a schooner, we had two great and swift boats from the Warao, and a few smaller dinghies. We could just leave.

"And you, Lasana?" I asked. "Will you go with us?"

She was surprised that I would even ask.

"I will."

"With the baby?"

"With the baby."

But though the clan was firmly opposed to Carapana, there was no unanimous opinion regarding me. The sorcerer's poisoned seed has fallen into more than one mind. Every now and then, I saw someone from the clan, seeing me from a distance, suddenly turn away so as not to meet me and, lurking behind a bush, suspiciously studying my movements. This and that formerly good companion now would look away, afraid to meet my gaze. None has become my enemy, but the venom of uncertainty as to my true nature had seeped into their soul. Who knew whether there was not this perverse *kanaima* soul in me after all?

Even in my closest circle, a shadow of doubt crept in. One day, I went into Lasana's hut, neighboring my own, to ask something of her. Quite naturally, I looked in on the sick child. When Lasana's mother saw this, she screamed. Like mad, she threw herself at the child, hiding it from me with her body, and with a shrill scream, ordered me to go away. My heart sank. I left.

I sat down at the threshold of my hut. In a few minutes, Arasibo came to me, limping, and crouched down by my side, almost brushing me sideways. There was an extraordinary silence in nature: steamy, heavy air stood still.

There was as yet no rain, but a heavy downpour hung over us. Puffed-up rain clouds rested on the tree tops. The thumping of the Serima drum, always the same—always the same for days—seemed louder than ever. Like an ominous muttering of a demon, the sound breathed a merciless eloquence and took on an unmistakable meaning. It announced death. We were both listening to the same thing and had the same thought. Arasibo nudged me in the side, lazily raised his hand towards Serima, and muttered out of his mouth as if mockingly:

"Stupid Kanaholo."

"What Kanaholo?"

"Ah," yawned the invalid, "the sorcerer's apprentice. Kanaholo. Stupid."

"Stupid?"

"Stupid."

After a longish while, he spoke again, in an undertone, as if to himself rather than to me:

"Stupid Kanaholo thinks that he is drumming your death. But he is s drumming someone else's death."

"I know, Lasana's boy's."

Arasibo screwed up his face, gurgled, then let out a muffled chuckle:

"No, not Lasana's boy. He's drumming the death of Carapana. He just doesn't know it yet."

"It's just words, Arasibo, just words," I smiled a pale smile.

"Carapana will die today... or tomorrow."

He said this so casually as if making an untimely joke. Or maybe I misunderstood him?

"What are you saying, Arasibo?"

"Carapana will die today. Or tonight, in the night."

There was a hidden note in his seemingly careless voice, a hard, stony note that alerted me. Only now did I look up at Arasibo's face and—was struck speechless. The gloomy numbness of his last days had gone somewhere. The old, familiar, steady hatred was pouring out of his eyes again. But apart from hate, there beamed from his face a devilish joy.

"What are you up to?" I straightened up, surprised.

He was amused by my surprise. A crooked grimace screwed up his face again. He clearly had something up his sleeve. He teased and lingered.

"By ten thousand devils, Arasibo, speak!"

"When our hunters go hunting, their darts are not always poisoned with *wurari*,[5] because there is no *wurari* in this forest. You have to buy it from a distant Carib tribe, the Makushi, and it's expensive, the bastards keep the prices high. But our own poison grows in our thicket, *kumarawa*, though it is not as strong as *wurari*. We use it because it kills, too."

"Talk to the purpose, Arasibo!"

"Am I not? Yet I say: *kumarawa* kills, too. Its leaves are nasty work. You touch a leaf with your paw, you will get skin ulcers, become delirious like drunk. Touch them more often, and you will die. Wicked business, that plant."

"Get to the point, Arasibo! Don't torture me!"

He threw me a long, biting glance full of idiotic delight at my impatience.

"What an impatient man you are, White Jaguar! We say about

---

[5] **Curare**: a common name for various alkaloid arrow poisons originating from plant extracts. Used as a paralyzing agent by indigenous peoples in Central and South America for hunting and for therapeutic purposes, curare only becomes active when it contaminates a wound. These poisons cause weakness of the skeletal muscles and, when administered in a sufficient dose, eventual death by asphyxiation due to paralysis of the diaphragm. Curare is prepared by boiling the bark of one of the dozens of plant sources, leaving a dark, heavy paste that can be applied to arrow or dart heads. In medicine, curare has been used as a treatment for tetanus and strychnine poisoning and as a paralyzing agent for surgical procedures.

men like you: bathed in boiling soup," he clicked, his tongue clattered merrily, he squinted his crossed eyes. "I wonder how you would feel, White Jaguar, if they put a *kumarawa* leaf in your bed every night. You would not know anything. You would moan, writhe with pain, your skin would become covered with eruptions, you would waste before our eyes. You would die. And it is just a tiny little leaf."

He unwrapped a piece of fabric, which he had held in his right hand, and raised it to my eyes to see: inside lay something tiny, greenish-gray: a half-dry, shriveled leaf.

"Do not touch it!" he breathed a warning. "This *kumarawa* looks dead, but it is still as deadly as a scorpion!"

And then, suddenly, as if he had had enough playfulness, he became serious, and he gurgled out in a sharp whisper, pointing to the poisonous leaf:

"I found this in Lasana's baby's mat."

He added, rising to his feet:

"Someone had tossed it in at night. The baby had to become ill."

"Who did it?" I asked stupidly because the answer was starting to dawn on me.

"Heh, heh. You think?"

I slapped my forehead in amazement. What a discovery! I grasped its significance in no time. If we can catch a sorcerer in the act—what a triumph! It would free me from terrible suspicions and would completely bury him. With mad joy, I seized Arasibo by the shoulders and shook him wildly, dancing and roaring. I grunted breathlessly:

"How did you discover this, man?"

"Well... I thought about it. I looked. And I asked the jaguar eye."

"And the kid... Can the kid be saved?"

"Yes. It will be saved."

I grabbed the little monster by the shoulders and crushed him to my chest.

"You wizard! You brainman! You wonderworker!"

Once we settled down a little and came back to reality, the question arose: what to do next? Convene a secret council of friends? Whom? Manauri, Arnak, Vagura and no one else?

Miguel?

"No. Only Arawaks. This is tribal business."

"And Lasana?"

"Lasana? Yes, of course."

Our friends were not far away: on the river. They were getting our schooner ready for a hasty departure in case of an attack. They dropped their work and came immediately. After we summoned Lasana, we secreted ourselves in my hut—Pedro was not around. And now Arasibo revealed to all the history of his discovery. Their initial bewilderment turned to exuberant joy, as had mine. A heavy weight fell from our hearts, but at the same time, we realized that now we were facing the hardest task: a life-and-death trial with the sorcerer.

"Death! His death!" repeated Manauri through clenched teeth.

We assumed that Carapana tossed poison into the baby's cot every second or third night, and since the *kumarawa* leaf Aresibo had found was already wilted, we expected the sorcerer's visit that night.

We decided to keep watch in pairs, with a change at midnight.

"You don't," said Manauri. "Your wound is still not healed."

He was right: I hadn't fully recovered yet. But it didn't seem fair to exclude me at a decisive moment, so I was assigned as the third man to the first pair: Arnak and Arasibo.

"Let's establish one more thing," said the chief, after much consideration. "This is our perfect chance to kill him. Let's kill him. We must kill him!"

"We must!" snarled Arasibo.

"Anyone opposed?" asked Manauri, glancing at me vigilantly.

Arnak and Vagura shook their heads to indicate consent. I did, too. There was no other solution but his death.

"Allow me to watch with you!" begged Lasana.

"Watch—yes!" said Manauri. "But not with us, outside, but inside your hut, with your boy."

No one—no matter who—could possibly get wind of our plans. We asked Lasana to burn the baby's bedding and to put him to sleep on a new mat elsewhere in the hut, but in such a way that her mother wouldn't suspect anything.

In the evening, there was a torrential rain, torrential though short-lived. When it stopped, clouds still covered the sky. We were afraid that the night might be too dark to see anything, but no: the moon shone somewhere above clouds, and its light filtered through and lit the night a little.

Lasana's hut stood some fifty paces from the water's edge, turned away from the water, with its entrance facing the forest. There was nothing growing around the hut except for some trampled grass and a few bushes left over from clearing the forest. The open space and partial darkness were perfect for our purposes.

As weapons, we all took short Arawak maces of hardwood, and in addition, Arnak and Arasibo took knives. I took a pistol loaded with lead shot to shoot at close range. Having agreed various voice signals that we were to use to communicate, we took our positions as soon as night fell. Arnak hid at the back of the hut, facing the river, Arasibo and I on the opposite side, a few paces from the entrance.

Inside the hut, Lasana stayed awake, waiting.

Several times, the rain pounded on our heads in short, violent torrents, and then it became almost completely dark, and the air invariably warm and steamy. There was no helping that, and there was no helping the boredom of the slowly passing hours.

Constantly piercing the darkness with strained eyes tired and eventually dulled the mind. In addition, the uncertainty of whether the enemy would appear that night did not make our vigil any easier. From time to time, we succumbed to delusions of the senses. Strange voices seemed to come from the edge of the forest or the river bank, and mysterious shadows darted in the gloom. Sometimes, they were dogs, or domesticated animals. At other times, bats, or wild reptiles from the thicket, or giant insects, or some other unknown bogeymen of the night.

Midnight was approaching, and I was slowly getting ready to leave and wake up my friends for the next watch when we heard behind the hut the croaking of a frog—Arnak's prearranged signal. He had noticed something.

I gripped my mace tighter in my right hand and the handle of the pistol in my left. All was as it had been all night. We could barely make out the corners of the hut, shaded by the overhanging eave, outlined darker against the slightly lighter background. Suddenly, it seemed to me that against this background, something moved to the left, as if a creature stood at the corner or clung to it. I nudged Arasibo in the side and pointed to the enigmatic apparition.

He breathed soundlessly:

"He's here."

Yes, there was someone there, and it surely was not Arnak. In the evening, we had agreed that no one would leave his post unless there was a loud alarm. But the dark creature did not look like Carapana either: it seemed stocky and short, while the sorcerer's figure was tall and gaunt. The mysterious man moved very slowly towards the entrance of the hut. I was now sure that it was not Carapana. Were there perhaps two of them? Maybe the sorcerer was following behind? Seeing that Arasibo prepared to jump out, I secretly grabbed his arm.

"See?" I breathed in his ear. "Not Carapana!"

"No!" he admitted.

"We take him alive."

"Alive?" I heard disappointment and resistance in my companion's whisper. "Whatever for?"

There was no time for discussion. I squeezed Arasibo's shoulder and commanded him with a strangled growl:

"Alive! Don't you dare kill him!"

He broke away from me. With the knife in his right hand, he leaped forward. He jumped with an astonishing, incomprehensible agility of which no one would have ever suspected him. He had four, maybe five, steps to his target. But the enemy had been on his guard. Did something suspicious warn him, or did he hear our whispers? Whatever the cause, he jumped suddenly. The knife missed him. Arasibo's paws did not manage to grasp him: they slipped off the intruder's greased body.

Attacked, the intruder rushed towards the corner of the hut where I had first seen him, but that route was now closed: I blocked his path and whacked him with my mace straight on the head. I heard a mighty thump in the dark. Yet, not hard enough, the shadow stumbled but didn't fall. He turned left, leaped forward, and—fell straight into Arnak's arms. The two fell to the ground together. Again, I smashed him on the head, and Arnak jumped on him and pinned him to the ground.

"Take him alive!" I screamed at the top of my head.

"Can't hold him!" boomed Arnak. "The bastard is all slimy!"

He was still struggling like crazy, but there was no hope anymore. I put both hands around his neck and didn't let go, and Arnak grabbed his wrists and pulled them over his back until his joints cracked. He was naked, only tied with a waistband. And he had greased himself to make himself difficult to capture.

In the dark, we could not make out who he was, but we knew it was not Carapana. He ignored our questions.

Lasana came running with a piece of ship's rope, and we tied him like a Christmas ham. He was apparently alone. We found no one else.

"He came by boat!" breathed Arnak heavily. "I heard him as he jumped out of it."

"Was he alone?"

"Alone! I saw no one else!"

"Run to the boat! See if it is still there!"

It was.

As the struggle began, Lasana's mother, suddenly awakened, let out a deafening scream, thinking it was an attack. All the neighbors rose and came running from all directions with weapons in hand.

The alarm worked surprisingly well. Not half a minute passed when the first man arrived, and a minute later, all were there, all armed. Not one had forgotten his rifle. Our clan was a well-oiled war machine! I was proud of it—despite the excitement—my chest puffed up because their fighting readiness was largely due to my training.

Some, more prudent, brought hastily kindled torches or animal fat lamps. When their light fell on the face of the captive, stupefaction seized everyone: it was the juvenile sorcerer's apprentice, Kanaholo, a boy of less than fourteen and yet such an expert in the criminal profession.

When he defended himself, he was as agile as a monkey and had had a knife on him, but now bound, lying down on the ground, our powerless poisoner, he was terrified to his soul. Seeing so many faces contorted by rage above him, he thought that his final hour had come. And he was not very far from the truth.

Manauri explained to everyone in a loud voice exactly what had brought the young criminal here. As he revealed Carapana's wicked plot, the indignation against his apprentice grew, and the most angered were the women. At a certain moment, Lasana's mother jumped to the young man and wanted to scratch his eyes out.

"You murderer!" she raged. "You monster! You were going to kill an innocent child!"

It was hard to tear her away from him. But no one proposed to spare his life: many demanded to kill him on the spot. Such agitated minds could do irreparable damage, so it was necessary to control them and get as much information out of the boy as possible.

Meanwhile, Manauri ordered two large bonfires to be started, and he appointed a few youngsters to keep watch over them so that they would not go out. It became quite light, and now we could see the prisoner clearly.

In the first moments after overpowering him, there was nothing but insane terror on his face. But Kanaholo soon saw that he was not in immediate danger of death, and his eyes hardened. We saw in them his cunning—an obvious thing: the sorcerer had not chosen a fool for his apprentice and successor.

The prisoner was lying in an unnatural position, his right side to the ground, which at first gave the impression that he had been wounded, perhaps broke a limb. When we stretched him on his back, he immediately changed his position and returned to the previous one. This caught my attention. Was Kanaholo trying to hide something from our eyes under his right flank?

"Did you find any *kumarawa* on him?" I asked Arasibo, who was standing nearby.

"No, we haven't looked. We will wait till daylight, then search. He may have dropped it somewhere."

"That is most important! That will be irrefutable evidence of his guilt!"

"Yes, but now it is too dark to search."

"And did you find anything on him?"

Arasibo gave me an uncertain look. The captive, being quite naked, had no place to hide anything.

Manauri began to question him but accomplished nothing: the young man sank into stubborn silence and uttered not a word. People were standing around, thirty of us, maybe forty, men, women, even kids, fuming with anger, shaking with curiosity. They expected an explanation. They wanted proof of guilt, visible proof.

There were in the crowd assembled around the captive several people not of our clan, close neighbors, drawn to the commotion as much as the others. They were not enemies, but neither were they friends. So when they heard Manauri's accusations against Carapana, they became terrified. They recognized the power of their sorcerer, they were influenced by him: they did not think to discredit him rashly just because someone made an accusation against him. So they started whispering amongst themselves. And since Kanaholo remained silent, they approached Manauri with their doubts:

"You made heavy accusations. You spoke some bold words."

"I know what I said," replied the chief. "White Jaguar is innocent. He has a healthy soul. Carapana wants to destroy him, so he poisoned Lasana's child, used Kanaholo to throw *kumarawa* leaves in the baby's bed."

"Who has seen these leaves?!" they asked. "Are you talking about Arasibo, maybe? He is a cripple, a crank. He hates Carapana. He has made this up."

"He found a *kumarawa* leaf in the baby's mat!"

"And who showed it to you? Who found it? Arasibo?"

"Yes, Arasibo!"

"So he found it and brought it to you to show you? He could have brought the leaf from the forest!"

"And Kanaholo?" yelled Manauri, outraged. "What is he doing here, at the sick child's hut?"

"We don't know? But neither do you!"

"I know! Tomorrow, we will find *kumarawa* leaves somewhere on the ground! You will see!"

"Yes, but who had put it there? Maybe Arasibo did?"

The scoundrels in charge of the fires apparently stopped adding fuel, for the flames subsided a little. I was standing closest to the prisoner. His hands were tied behind his back, and he was lying on them. As soon as the fires died down, it did not escape my notice that the young man, taking advantage of the semi-darkness, began to make mysterious efforts with his hands as if to grasp something hidden under his right side. Soon, new flames shot up from the fires, and the prisoner froze. Then, I made an interesting discovery: I noticed an object protruding slightly from the side of the youth. Wasn't that the tip of a piece of a bamboo tube? Arawaks commonly used bamboo tubes to carry small things. Now, I had no doubt why Kanaholo was lying in such an odd position: he was trying to hide something under his body, something that might reveal his secret.

I was speaking to Arnak to warn him of my discovery when Arasibo, who had left us for a while, came running with the jaguar's skull. He drove a spear into the ground so that it was bent over the captive and placed the skull on the end of it, its open socket staring at the boy. In the flickering light, the skull seemed to come alive, the predatory fangs seemed to move, and the black eye cavity cast an eerie menace on the villain. The impression was powerful. The youngster shuddered, and his eyes opened so wide in terror that they nearly popped out of his head. He remained stubbornly silent, but he was clearly seized with fear and was unable to hide that.

"Now you will tell us all!" boomed Arasibo. "Speak, or the spirit of the jaguar will tear you apart!"

Looking at Arasibo, I had no doubt that he would have preferred to rip the sorcerer's apprentice apart with his own bare hands, but his magical interrogation achieved nothing. The captive only pursed his lips and remained as silent as the grave.

"You won't get anything out of him!" someone from among the sorcerer's supporters snorted as if to encourage the prisoner.

Manauri sent a messenger to Kanaholo's father in Serima, hoping that perhaps the sight of his father would break him.

"It's going badly!" murmured Arnak to me. "He's a stubborn rogue! We will lose this confrontation."

"Who will lose? You lose your hope so easily, Arnak?"

"We will not be able to prove his guilt!"

"I do not recognize my old friend Arnak. Giving up so easily? Before such a kid? Are you blind? Arnak? Can't you see?"

My friend sensed cheerfulness in my voice—as I sensed it once in Arasibo's voice. Arnak looked up at me:

"Do you see something?"

"I do."

And I confided to him my guess concerning the strange wriggling movements of the prisoner and his attempts to hide a bamboo tube under him.

Arnak's eyes lit up, though he retained control over his facial expression. After a while, he became convinced of the validity of my observations.

"The devil is hiding something! Now I see it!" he whispered and looked at me with admiration. "I can see your sight has returned, and so has your wit! No, we will not lose this encounter. But let *me* reveal what we have discovered!"

"Yes! Go ahead!"

Arnak explained briefly to Manauri, Vagura, and Arasibo what he planned to do, then ordered the fires to be stoked and summoned all the more prominent men, both of our clan and from Serima, especially the doubters. When he had everything ready, he announced in a thunderous and solemn voice that no one could cheat the jaguar eye. The eye had revealed Carapana's criminal intentions and told us where Kanaholo hides his *kumarawa* leaves.

"Do you want to know where?" he asked triumphantly, looking at the assembled men in turn.

"Show us," said several voices.

Arnak leaned over the captive, took him by the armpits, and, with one jerk, stood him up.

"Do you see?" he shouted fiercely in a sudden surge of anger.

And we all saw: on the string girding the youngster's waist, at his right buttock, hung a bamboo container.

"What do you have in this bamboo?" boomed Arnak at the captive.

He was no longer the dashing, hardy sorcerer apprentice. He was a kid, frightened out of his wits, trembling with emotion and fear.

"What do you have in the bamboo tube?" Now, Manauri repeated the question sharply and commandingly. "Talk!"

Kanaholo muttered something unintelligible under his breath. His sudden tremors only confirmed to us that something very important was in the bamboo tube. Arasibo jumped to the captive, tore off the tube from his waist, took out the stopper, and, right in front of our eyes, poured its contents into the palm of his hand—in his excitement, he didn't care about the burns.

We saw three crumpled leaves.

"*Kumarawa!*" the invalid whinnied in a high-pitched shriek, now looking more like a demon from hell than a man. He stretched out his hand in the direction of the bonfire and ordered everyone to take a closer look.

"Is this *kumarawa* or not?" he asked each in turn, and in his unbridled excitement, his throat croaked, buzzed, and whistled.

He knew that in that one moment, everything was at stake: he could now destroy the dominion of the sorcerer, his fierce enemy. Victory, hate, and madness flashed on his trembling face. Like a man possessed, he wheezed to everyone in turn:

"Say: is this *kumarawa*?"

"It is *kumarawa*," one by one, confirmed the members of our clan.

The others said nothing, closed in on themselves, but they saw it, recognized it. They could not deny it. Lasana's mother pushed through the crowd with a white mat in her hand.

"Throw the leaves here!" she ordered the invalid. "Or they will make you sick!"

Arasibo threw the leaves on the mat, then took the mat around, shoving it in everyone's face.

Meanwhile, Kanaholo, whom Arnak threw to the ground again, was certain that the last moment of his life had come, and he was shaking like a leaf in the wind.

"Look at the jaguar!" boomed Manauri at him, "and talk if your life is dear to you. Talk!"

"I will... I will!" sobbed the captive.

"Who sent you here?"

He mumbled something.

"Who?!"

"Carapana."

"Speak louder for all to hear. Who sent you here?"

"Carapana! The sorcerer!"

"And he gave you these leaves of *kumarawa*?"

"He did!"

"And what did he order you to do with them?"

"He ordered me to put them in Lasana's baby's bed while all were sleeping."

"And how many times have you done this?"

"Three times. This is the fourth."

"And did Carapana want the child to die?"

"Yes! He wanted the child to die."

"In order to then blame White Jaguar's soul?"

But at that moment, the captive choked with horror and burst into uncontrollable spasms, crying. But we had said enough. The people had heard him. They understood. Carapana's crime had come to light. No one could doubt it anymore.

The boy's father arrived, brought by the messenger. His presence was no longer necessary as the boy had already confessed. It was evident that Aripai—that was the name of the captive's father—was a rather kind-hearted creature, a man with a calm and kind disposition, who probably had no inkling of his son's doings. Kanaholo had to repeat to him what he had testified to us. The father listened gloomily, greatly depressed, blankly looking now at us, now at his son.

"What will you do with him?" he asked in the end.

A few demanded death for the young culprit, and in demanding it, they invoked the ancient customs of the tribe. But most did not judge him so severely, considering that Kanaholo was only a tool in the hands of the real culprit. These people did not wish to kill the boy, and when I was asked my opinion, I sided with them. So we cut the youngster's bonds and sent him away with his father.

"Look well after him!" I said to Aripai. "See to what he does. And do not entrust him to uncertain hands again!"

The Indian was pleased that we left Kanaholo alive, but his face did not light up.

"My son... my son is no longer in my care. I had given him to the sorcerer. He has to go back to him."

The next day, the sad news spread through the Arawak settlement that Kanaholo suddenly died. The wretched boy was found dead at the edge of the forest near Serima, with no sign of violence.

People of our clan took the news very calmly: they expected that this would happen, for such a punishment befalls all who betray a sorcerer's secret, even if they do it through no fault of their own.

Repartimiento

Kanaholo's capture in the act and his testimony freed me from the foolish suspicions of having a *kanaima* soul, but they did not touch the real criminal. The cunning sorcerer knew how to weasel out. His authority in the tribe was formidable. Everything pointed to his crime, even Kanaholo's death, and yet Serima feared the sorcerer so much that they did not dare revolt—or even speak up against him. Rather, they preferred to give credence to the sorcerer's unbelievable story that Kanaholo had been framed: that who knew by what criminal means a false confession was forced out of him by our clan and that the poisonous leaves had somehow been sneakily planted on the youngster. In a word, Carapana twisted the whole business around, and some of Serima's men, out of fear or convenience, agreed to go along with this nonsense.

There were heated discussions among my close friends about what to do. We came to the conclusion that the sorcerer's influence, though tarnished, was still overwhelming, and it seemed to us impossible to kill him without causing a bloody civil war in the tribe. So we returned to the idea of leaving Serima and began our last preparations for this purpose. Now, the whole clan readied for departure: everyone had had enough of Carapana's tricks. In these last days, the ties of friendship between the clan and me became even closer: friendship and trust intertwined our destinies. It soon turned out that Serima was no longer what it used to be—a homogeneous, compact community of like-minded people. When word of our intention to leave reached the village, many Serima residents expressed the desire to leave along with us. They didn't want to remain under the control of a dangerous sorcerer.

They were free to leave: by established Arawak custom, no one had the right to prevent them from wandering off. But such a prospect, of course, greatly angered Carapana and alarmed the chief Coneso. Hoping to prevent the division of their tribe—something which both had feared from the moment of our arrival—the sorcerer hatched a monstrous plan to attack us and kill us all, and if not all, then at least the leading members of our clan: Manauri, Lasana, and even Pedro included. Fortunately, kind people warned us in advance, so we were on our guard and watched all movement in Serima, never letting our weapons out of hand. And we hastened our preparations for departure.

And in this tense moment, an unexpected event took place, which thwarted our plans.

One day, about two hours after sunrise, two inhabitants of Serima rushed out of the woods separating their settlement from ours and, with signs of excitement, ran towards us. It was not a trick, as we thought at first, and when the running Indians saw us from afar, they started shouting strange words.

"Do I hear them correctly?" I asked Arnak with a sudden bad feeling. "Are they saying... Spaniards?"

"So they are," replied my friend in an audibly changed voice.

We raised an alarm, and soon, all our clansmen were at our side.

Meanwhile, the runners got to us, panting and barely able to stay on their feet with exhaustion. They looked pitiful: they hadn't just been running, but they were clearly in utter terror.

"Spaniards! Spaniards!" they breathed heavily and pointed back.

"Spaniards... There!..."

"Where?" Manauri yelled back at them.

"In Serima! They came! They landed! Spaniards!"

That was terrible news. A word like a thunderclap: Spaniards! After all, all my clan had been enslaved by the Spaniards once—all except Arnak and Vagura, who had been English slaves. Spaniards—

that word sounded like a curse to any Indian, and wherever we had met them—on Ribinson's Island, on the *llanos* near Mount Vulture, everywhere we had had to defend ourselves against their attacks. Many of us trembled in our hearts.

"Have they attacked you?" asked Manauri. "Did they kill someone?"

"No, no, they didn't attack."

"Was there any fighting?"

"No."

"Have all Arawaks escaped from Serima?"

"No! The Spaniards surprised us. Only some escaped."

"And they didn't attack you?"

"No, no. They didn't attack. But they have landed, they are armed, they look hostile."

"How many are there?"

The messengers, still catching their breath, could not agree on the number of the arrivals: one said there were as many as the fingers on both hands, another that there were ten times more.

"No!" the first contradicted him. "The Spaniards are few, the rest are Indians!"

"There are Indians with them?"

"Yes!"

"What tribe?"

"Don't know, some strange tribe."

"On how many boats did they come?"

"On five boats."

"Big ones?"

"Yes, five big *itauba*."

"Not five," corrected the second runner. "On three *itauba*."

And what do they want? Do you know?

They didn't know, they had no clue. The only thing they could say was that the Spaniards, although they did not start fighting,

Arawak Indians, P.J.Benoit, *Reis door Suriname*, 1839

behaved imperiously and defiantly, like rulers, like someone who comes with a threat, not as a friendly house guest. They exuded danger and misfortune. They sowed fear.Having exchanged glances with Manauri and Arnak, I told everyone present to run and get their weapons and immediately present themselves in front of my hut. Fortunately, almost the whole clan was at hand, and soon, all stood at the ready. Pedro was by my side. When he heard that his countrymen had arrived, all the blood drained from his face, and he turned as white as a sheet. I nudged him with my elbow.

"What do you say to that?" I said to him in the Spanish he had taught me. "Your countrymen!"

Pedro was in such shock that he probably could not count to five at the moment. On his pleasant, open face, which normally beamed so much reasonable confidence, I could now see boundless stupefaction.

"If..." he stammered at last, full of fearful uncertainty. "Whether...?"

"But of course! Haven't I told you already? You are free, and you can go with them if you like."

"Oh, *señor*, thank you!"

"Oh, Pedro!" I laughed. "Are we suddenly such strangers that you have to *señor* me?"

"No! No... Forgive me, Yan... Everything's upside down in my head."

"Hey, Pedrino, keep your head straight because we both need it! Maybe you can guess what they want?"

But Pedro couldn't say anything. Since Serima lay quite hidden, a few miles from the confluence of the Imataca and the Orinoco, and Imataca was not a much-frequented waterway, we had to assume that the Spaniards had not arrived by chance, in passing, but had a clear and predetermined goal.

"From where could they have arrived?" I asked Pedro.

I told him to bring the map he had been drawing for several weeks. He unrolled it for us to see. On it, near the top of the map—

that is, in the north of the country—there was the line of the lower reaches of the Orinoco, running horizontally, left to right. And some distance away, at the bottom (and therefore in the south) and almost parallel to it, ran the line of the Cuyuni River. Each river had many tributaries, and between the two river systems stretched a mountain range, which Pedro had called Mount Imataca, and through which he had carefully drawn several Indian paths running north to south, connecting the Orinoco and the Cuyuni.

"Where are Spaniards here?"

From where we were, all the way to the mouth of the Orinoco, there had been no Spaniards, as we had seen ourselves. So, these newcomers must have come from Trinidad. Or from Margarita.

"From that far away?"

"I don't know, Yan! Maybe it's a pursuit? Or maybe they came from the upper Orinoco? There have been settlements there for quite a while. If so, then those Spanish had not come by way of the sea but downriver, from New Granada."

"Do they have many soldiers there?"

"There is military there, that's for sure, but whether many, I don't know. There is the town of Angostura,[6] I have told you. It has been there for centuries. I don't think it is very big and I am not really sure what the Spanish do there. There are several Dominican missions thereabouts with their own land grants and praying Indians."

"How far from here?"

"Angostura? I am not sure exactly. Maybe hundred, hundred-fifty miles?"

While I was talking to Pedro, all our warriors assembled together, and as they all more or less knew the Spanish language, they listened attentively to our conversation. There were a few Indians from Serima, too. They did not understand a word of Spanish, but when they heard the name Angostura, there was a lively commotion between them. They knew the word. They approached, and one of

---

[6] Present day Ciudad Bolivar, first founded in 1576.

them said to me:

"White Jaguar! We know that Angostura-place. There are Spaniards there! They were here recently, maybe two dry seasons ago, shortly after we arrived on the Imataca. They discovered us, and they said that they would be back."

"Tell White Jaguar what else they did!" reminded him another Indian.

"What else did they do?" I asked.

"Ah, right!" he laughed. "They gave Coneso many different items. Not as gifts, no. They said that they would come back and we would have to pay for them then. Maybe they're back now to collect the payment?"

"What sort of things were they?"

"All kinds of things... Shirts and pants—what the Spanish wear, but old and torn. And shoes, but many with holes, or only one. And dried meat from their cows. The meat was smelly, full of worms—we gave it to the dogs. And they gave us several of these strange knives. You have such a knife, White Jaguar! In the morning, you stand before your hut and scrape your chin with it."

"A razor! They gave you razors? But you don't have any hair on your chins!"

The Indian looked at me with astonishment as if I had made an extraordinarily perceptible observation. Then he exploded in childish gaiety.

"And who says they were for scraping our chins?" his mouth twisted in mockery.

"What were they for, then?"

"For nothing! They were blunt and chipped, many were broken or rusty, they did not cut even soft twigs. They crumbled in our fingers."

"So why did you take them?"

"We had to. We didn't want to, but they forced us, saying that otherwise, they would take hostages."

"Take men into captivity?"

"Yes. They were not merchants, Yan. Not really. They were sent by the Spanish chief in Angostura, the *corregidor*. And they came with soldiers, with loaded guns."

The Indian's story struck me as preposterous, but Pedro, who had already learned something of the Arawak language, said that the Indian's story sounded likely. One of the Spanish systems of exploiting the Indians was the so-called *repartimiento*. In a *repartimiento*, the *corregidor*, or district prefect, forced a tribe, especially one residing in a secluded area, to buy miscellaneous goods, usually of little use, sometimes completely useless, but always at terribly inflated prices. The Indians had to buy those things, whether they wanted to or not. They did not have to pay immediately, only later, after a year or two, and, of course, paid in kind with the products of the land, of the forest, or of some handicraft. And if they could not repay the debt to the satisfaction of the *corregidor*, some were then taken as punishment: usually, a number of young men to work on Spanish haciendas or in the mines.

"According to the law, they are taken for a certain period of time, two, three, or five years," Pedro continued his explanation. "But in reality, hardly any of them ever comes back. They die from exhaustion, disease, or sadness. Or are retained by their employer for life. I have seen such people more than once. Poor bastards."

"And do you suppose these are the envoys of the *corregidor*? To collect their payment?"

"I don't know."

Manauri had already sent two scouts to Serima to report on the movements of the Spanish and to warn us immediately if they approached. Our schooner stood on the river and would make a tasty treat for the Spanish mauls. It was not visible from Serima, but the Spaniards would spot it as soon as they went around the bend in the river. Nor should the Spanish see our African friends.

I nodded to Manauri, Arnak, and Miguel to come aside with

me. When we found ourselves alone, I explained my plan to them: Miguel and his five companions would immediately move the schooner up the Imataca: it was a good moment for it, for the tide was rising. About a mile up the river, the current had cut a nice round bay on a bend, and they should hide the schooner there.

All the Africans should arm themselves with guns, pistols, and swords and take Dolores with them. They would remain on board, stay as quiet as mice, and guard the ship.

My friends agreed, but Manauri suggested a small change to my plan: he said that the schooner should be taken even further upriver. More than three miles up was the second bay, called Potaro. It would be better to hide the ship there as it would be even further from the Spanish.

"Excellent!" I said and turned to Miguel: "Most importantly, No one must see your departure, understand? You should be able to get away unseen since everyone's attention is now on Serima, around the bend from here."

I divided the other men of our clan into two teams, one under the command of Arnak and one under Vagura. And I was about to set out for Serima with Manauri and Pedro when one of our scouts came running from Serima to say that Coneso was coming.

"He's running!"

"Coneso is running? The chief is running?"

"Yes! Running!"

Coneso was indeed running. Not as fast as my two scouts, for he was heavier and older than they, but he was running—clearly in a hurry to get to us. To Manauri. His usual dash had disappeared from his face, the pomp was gone. He was just a panting fat man in trouble.

"Manauri!" he groaned. "We need you! Quick! Quick! You have to help us!"

"I will help you, but how?" flustered Manauri.

"For the life of me, I can't communicate with these men! You speak Spanish."

"So I do."

"You have to explain to them! Tell them! We are not a rich tribe. They demand so much. They are out of their minds! We can never deliver what they ask! That's what you have to tell them!"

"And what do they demand?"

"Everything! Ask what they do not demand; that will be easier to say! To satisfy them, the whole tribe would have to toil year-round in the field, and in the forest, and on the river, and even then, it wouldn't be enough! May the river swallow the Spanish! We have no money to pay, either, and they demand that, too!"

"How many are there?" I interjected myself into the conversation. Coneso paused to collect his thoughts.

"Of the Spaniards, there are ten. Or twelve. And at their head is this Don Esteban, envoy of the *corregidor* of Angostura. They are all armed up to their teeth!"

"And the Indians?"

"Good five times ten. They're Chayma. Rowers. All are armed like Indians, like us."

"What sort of Indians are they?"

"They live near Angostura. They're praying Indians. They live on a Dominican mission."

"Are these the same Spaniards who were here two dry seasons ago?"

"The same!"

"And imposed on you so much broken and useless stuff you didn't want?"

"Yes! How do you know?"

"I know."

So the matter was clear: it was *repartimiento*. The Spaniards have arrived not to kill or conquer but to collect tribute. But what would they do when they didn't get paid? Will they not pounce on the Indians to take slaves? Coneso feared the same. Hence his terror and desperate search for a way out.

Looking around in a panic, he suddenly noticed Pedro. I saw an idea light up in his head. He approached the youth, put his arm around him, and his face suddenly flashed with overbearing kindness.

"You are our captive, yes?" he smiled at him coaxingly. "Have we treated you badly? Do you have anything to complain about? Unfairness or injustice?"

Confused, Pedro did not know how to reply.

"No," he mumbled.

"Well, you have nothing to complain about! I now return your freedom to you, but you have to speak to Don Esteban in our defense! We will return his countryman to him, and he will forgive us our debt!"

"If you want... I can..."

"Listen, Coneso!" I interrupted their conversation. "Do not forget that Pedro is *my* prisoner."

"Is that not all the same?" the chief glanced at me sideways, anger flashing in his eyes.

"No, it is not the same."

"And do you want to keep Pedro in captivity?"

"No. I have granted him his freedom. Pedro is now free."

"But you forbid him to go to Don Esteban?"

"Not at all! But I have released him without condition, and I am not going to change my word now."

"And do you object if Pedro speaks for us?" Coneso jabbered on.

"I don't want to quarrel with you," I replied with a shrug.

And then I saw how his eyes, which had become dull for a moment, now, as if under the influence of a new thought, flickered with a strange, cunning flash which he immediately suppressed. He cast a glance in the direction of the river where our schooner stood, though it was invisible from our position since a hillock separated us from the shore. Coneso instantly diverted his gaze, but he had already betrayed himself by that glance and by the cunning expression, which now crawled out all over his face.

It was clear: Coneso had thought about the schooner. He was scheming, the wretched traitor. Since Pedro was not available to trade, he decided he had another gift for the Spanish: our good, proud ship. How grateful the Spaniards would be to him for such a generous gift!

As soon as I guessed his filthy intentions, I whispered to Arnak in English to go stealthily to the river and order the Africans to stop all work and hide themselves somewhere. Then I jumped over to Coneso and, pointing to the jaguar skull on the pole, yelled furiously in his ear:

"Look! Look at the eye of the jaguar! It tells me everything!"

The men standing around us, terrified by my explosion, looked now at me, now at the jaguar skull in utter astonishment. Coneso became abashed.

"The skull reveals to me," I said, "that you are plotting betrayal! You want to save yourself at our expense! Don't you dare!"

"The skull! The skull?!" mumbled the chief, terrified. "The magical skull?!"

"Yes! The magical skull! It revealed to me exactly what disgusting plot you are hatching!"

His confusion only confirmed my suspicions. Leaving him alone, I called Manauri aside. I recommended that he go to Serima with Coneso to help him negotiate with the Spanish as Coneso asked, but take with him a bright companion from our clan, fluent in Spanish. His task was to inform me from time to time about the state of affairs and the progress of the negotiations with the Spaniards.

Soon, Coneso, Manauri, and the third fellow left, but before they did, Coneso as if in passing, approached the edge of the river to cast a glance at our ship. I didn't leave his side. The chief had had a chance to cool down and master his emotions. On seeing our ship anchored in its usual place, shrouded in silence, as if forgotten by men, an expression of satisfaction appeared on the face of the chief—and on mine as well.

Shortly after they left, I went to the edge of the woods to survey Serima with my telescope. The newcomers had brought three large rowing boats, large dugouts commonly used on the Orinoco. Near the boats sat crowded together a few dozen Indian rowers armed with bows and maces.

A little further on, I saw the Spaniards. They, too, stuck together, though some of them were lying down and appeared to be resting or sleeping while others stood guard. Long guns stood arranged in trestles right next to the group.

As I could see through the glass, they were all bearded men, hairy, mean swashbucklers. Their souls and consciences seemed little brighter than their beards. Their commander, Don Esteban, as Coneso called him, was not to be seen anywhere. Evidently, he was talking to the chief and Manauri under the roof of one of the huts.

The Spanish and the Indians seemed calm, but they were clearly on guard and kept their weapons to hand. Seeing nothing else worth interest, I returned to our settlement.

Two hours later, around noon, I received the first message from Serima: it was difficult to reach an agreement. The Spaniards demanded a huge payment and threatened strict penalties in the event of refusal. Worse, they had learned about the existence of my clan. Worse yet, a helpful soul had whispered to them that we were a lineage of former slaves escaped from Spanish captivity and had killed many Spaniards. The presence of Pedro would have made it impossible to hide from the newcomers all the details of our past and the battles we had fought, but it pained me greatly that a vile person among the Arawaks was ready to inform on us. The faithless dog did not hesitate to betray his own brothers to a common enemy.

Had Coneso fallen so low?

Meanwhile, the schooner raised anchor, cleared the shore, and made smoothly for its hiding place. In a couple of hours, I received word that it had safely ensconced itself in its bay. Before its departure, I had all firearms brought ashore as well as paper, pen, and ink.

"Pedro!" I summoned the boy. "There is a Spanish book describing funny adventures of a freakish knight... Do you know it?"

"I think you mean *Don Quixote*."

"Yes, exactly! What is the name of the creator of this book?"

"Miguel de Cervantes y Saavedra."

And now, with the help of Pedro, I wrote a letter to the Spaniards:

> *Illustrious* señor Commandante!
> *I use the happy occasion of your arrival in our parts of the country to convey to you my greetings and my due respect.*
> *At the same time, it is my great pleasure to entrust to your care a respectable young Spanish nobleman, Pedro Martinez, who, due to a capricious sequence of events, regrettable but of the cause of which we were entirely innocent, has been my traveling companion. I humbly ask you, sir, to take him under your protection.*
> *Moreover, I allow myself to add an earnest request that you show my friends, the Arawak Indians of Serima, the famous Spanish magnanimity worthy of a representative of the nation that gave the genius of Miguel Cervantes Saavedra to the world.*
> *Please deign to accept my most respectful salutations,*
> *John Bober*

"Is this Cervantes Saavedra thing okay? Is it not too stuck up?" I asked Pedro. "Perhaps I am writing to some uncultured lowlife?"

"It doesn't hurt to try," replied the boy, in a glowing mood that his fate was taking such a positive turn, though I could see in him a little sadness, too, at the prospect of our parting.

I sent Pedro to Serima with the letter, asking him to remain among his countrymen. Both I and my clan had all come to like him, and especially our cheerful Vagura. So, as much as we hoped that this was not our final farewell, we all hugged him tenderly.

Night expedition

And now Lasana's mother came to me with an enigmatic expression and whispered the following: she had just returned from the forest where she had been gathering herbs. At the edge of the thicket, she was accosted by old Katawi, an old man who lived at the mouth of Our River (Imataca), where it emptied into the Great River (Orinoco), and he asked her to ask me to come to him in the forest. He had something very important to tell me but asked that we meet in total secrecy.

"Why doesn't he come here?" I asked suspiciously, scenting a trick which the woman did not.

"No. He says it is too important."

"Who is this Katawi? Do you know him?"

"Oh, yes, I know him! He is a good man, and he hates Carapana. Go to him because it is urgent!"

I asked Arnak and Vagura. They did not know Katawi, but they had full confidence in the old woman's wisdom and foresight.

"Let's go, the three of us!" suggested Vagura, his eyes burning at the prospect of an adventure.

We went, armed as if to hunt. We met Katawi at the agreed place. He was an old Indian, though still spritely and quick, and he lived by fishing. His hut stood alone about five miles downriver from us. As honest and trustworthy as he seemed, I decided to move a few hundred paces from the meeting place as a precaution, keeping a close eye on the thicket. Nobody followed us.

"Speak, Katawi!" I said to him when we settled in the shade of a large tree.

Katawi may have been a brave fisherman, but he was a poor orator. We had to fish for facts in his story as if sifting it through a sieve. As the facts emerged, we became more and more astonished.

At dawn of that day, Katawi had been on the Great River (Orinoco) and saw emerging from the morning mist five strange boats. They were the so-called *itauba,* or "mighty boats," hewn from a single trunk of the *itauba* tree. Hence the name. They came up the Great River (Orinoco), and there were Spaniards on them because he heard them in the dark giving orders to their Indian oarsmen in their language.

Opposite where Katawi was hiding, a small island loomed near the shore, and two *itauba* landed there. Soon, the other three boats continued their journey and entered the mouth of the Imataca River, and the fisherman later learned that they were now in Serima. But the two other boats, the boats that remained on the island, aroused his curiosity.

Namely, when the fog lifted in the morning, Katawi saw many prisoners, maybe three times ten, lying side by side in one *itauba*, all hog-tied with bast. In order to get a better look, he climbed to the top of a tree, and then he realized that they were all Warao.

Since the prisoners lay tied up, the Spaniards did not leave many guards with them: there were just two Spaniards and two Indians. Katawi observed them for a long time but did not see any more guards.

"What do you think? Will they leave that island soon?" I asked the fisherman.

"It didn't seem to me like they were getting to leave. They were setting up camp when I left."

"They won't leave until those in Serima rejoin them," Vagura said.

"I think you are right! And that other boat? You said, Katawi, that they had two *itauba* there," I asked next. "One was with prisoners. And the other? Was it empty?"

"No. She was filled to the brim. There was only enough room for a few rowers in the front and in the back."

"Filled with what?"

"I don't know because everything was covered with mats. But I think probably food for the whole group because if you count all the men—the Spanish, their Indians, and the prisoners—there are maybe ten times ten."

"And are you sure the prisoners are Warao?"

"You can kill me if I am wrong!"

Even while he still talked, I made the decision to come to the aid of the Warao.

I remembered what Pedro had told me about the *repartimiento* system. I guessed that the Warao had not been able to satisfy the Spanish demand for payment, and the Spanish took the thirty into slavery.

"We had sworn a solemn covenant with the Warao," I reminded my companions. "They are like brothers to us now. We must come to their aid."

"I wouldn't go *asking* the Spanish to release them," Vagura warned.

"I wasn't thinking about *asking*," I replied in a firm voice. "We'll just cut them free!"

My friends almost jumped for joy. Even the normally reserved Arnak got carried away.

"Katawi!" I turned to the old man. "You have done something very good and very noble. You deserve gratitude! But your work is not yet done! You still have to help us release these Warao, for we cannot do it without your help."

Katawi was a simple fisherman and he didn't show great enthusiasm for heroic deeds. He was confused:

"But can I help you?"

"Yes! You will show us the way to the island. We will do the rest!"

"Oh! That I can do!" Katawi said with visible relief.

"How do we get onto the island from the shore?"

"Easy. Very easy. I have two small bark boats. The distance is very close."

"How many men can fit in your two boats?"

"Six. Maybe seven."

"Very well. There will be six of us plus you, the seventh. We'll go as soon as it gets dark."

Katawi was too important a link in the whole enterprise to be left out of sight even for a moment. Besides, he still had the important task of describing the island to us, a momentous thing, considering that we would first see it in the dead of the night. So, without asking his say so, we took him with us to our village, prudently avoiding strangers' huts along the way. By a roundabout path and the riverside bush, we arrived at our settlement. We made him sit in a dark corner of my hut and gave him one of our warriors for company.

It seemed important to me that someone who spoke Warao should join our expedition. In this, Katawi gave us excellent advice: he said that the father of the unfortunate Kanaholo, Aripai, had married a woman of the Warao tribe and spoke their language. And Aripai was friendly to us. I immediately sent a messenger for him and another to Manauri with a firm order to try by all means to dissuade the Spaniards from leaving Serima that day.

Less than two hours later, Aripai arrived, and with him, a messenger with the news that the Spaniards had no intention of leaving today. Aripai, drawn into the conspiracy, quickly agreed to participate in the night mission.

When, during these feverish preparations, there was a moment of peace, a strange reverie engulfed me: how the events had piled up in the last few hours, how much uncertainty and anxiety had arisen! The Arawaks had divided into two unfriendly camps, and who knew what iniquities our tribesmen were plotting against us? A mortal danger hung over us in the form of the Spaniards, ready any moment, on any whim, to pounce on us to take slaves. The sorcerer Carapana was perhaps even now lurking about with some new ambush against me. Chief Coneso, shaken and frightened, was perhaps plotting to betray us to the Spanish. Our schooner was at risk—was it well concealed, and would Miguel defend it if attacked? And this new trouble with the Warao prisoners and the planned expedition by night, which, if it failed, might lead to our downfall! All the threads of this intricate situation were concentrated in my hand: tangled, twisted, and soon, I would be the first to see which one would break first and bring misfortune upon us. How easy it was to stumble and break!

My head was pounding from all this, and my thoughts were fuzzy, but I regained my peace and comfort as soon as I looked at the yard in front of my hut: there, ten warriors of our clan squatted under arms, ready for everything and anything, awaiting orders. They were calm and resolute, and among them were my unwavering friends, Arnak and Vagura. So who would win? There was a moment of silence but no time to get lost in thought: from the forest, ran towards us at top speed an Indian, whom I had posted there on guard.

"Seven Spaniards coming!" he fell among us with the news. "All heavily armed!"

"Are you sure they are coming here?"

"Yes! To us! They will soon be here!"

Our men took the message with composure worthy of respect. I ordered Arnak and Vagura to keep their men not far from my hut but separately, at some distance from each other, and to watch what sign I give them.

"And I? What should I do?" asked Arasibo. "What have I to do?"

"You go into my hut and guard the weapons we deposited there. And keep an eye on Katawi."

The Spaniards did indeed soon emerge from the woods. They were walking with a measured step straight for my hut, apparently known to them from descriptions. Muskets rested on their shoulders, like with an army on the march. When they approached me to within ten steps, they stood their matchlocks with the butts on the ground, and the eldest of them, stepping forward a little, said to me loftily, with exaggerated seriousness:

"*Señor capitan*! Don Esteban, our colonel, says he thanks you for your letter and, wishing to reciprocate your kind gesture, he politely invites you to pay him a visit in Serima."

It was evening. The sun would set in an hour. As soon as it did, I intended to set off on our mission downriver. It was too late for a visit that could keep me in Serima for who knows how long.

"Please thank your illustrious commander, Don Esteban, for his kind invitation and tell him that I will pay him a visit tomorrow morning."

"He begs you to pay him a visit today."

"And I beg him to wait until tomorrow."

A cloud came over the Spaniard's face, and he involuntarily tugged at his belt with an impatient flick of his hand.

"I received an order," he declared a little harder than so far, "to show you all due respect and to bring you to our camp today."

"And you seven will act as my guard of honor?" I asked, pretending to be pleasantly surprised.

"Yes! We will be your escort!"

To his surprise, I exploded with laughter:

"Ah, that is wonderful and very thoughtful of you! But, alas, I do not need your escort, for I have my own! Look here, look there!"

And I pointed to the right and to the left—to the teams of Arnak and Vagura. Their warriors stood in casual attitudes, negligent even, but gripped their matchlocks in hand and stared intently in our direction.

The Spaniard understood the eloquent meaning of their attitude and smiled a sour smile.

"It would not be my fault then," he said in a kinder voice, "if I could not carry out my orders today."

"No, indeed. It would not be your fault," I readily agreed with him.

He saluted and appeared ready to walk back to Serima.

"One more thing, *señor*! After sunset," I said, "no stranger is allowed to enter this clearing. My men are under strict orders to shoot at anyone who enters it. The residents in Serima know this, and I wish you to know this, also."

"Yes, *señor capitan*!"

They left, but not in the direction of Serima as I had expected, but towards the river, heading straight for the place where, until recently, our schooner had stood. So, Coneso had betrayed the existence of our ship to them! At my signal, Arnak's and Vagura's troops approached me just as the Spaniards were hurrying back from the river. They were very excited.

"Over there," exclaimed their chief, "there was a Spanish ship. Where is she?"

"She's not there," I replied dryly.

"What do you mean—she's not there?"

"Haven't you seen for yourself? She isn't there. And, at any rate, you appear to labor under a misapprehension, *señor*. She is not a Spanish ship. She is mine."

"But she formerly belonged to Spaniards!"

"Formerly, yes. But now, no longer."

"*Señor*!" objected the Spaniard with an edge in his voice. "We did not come here to suffer mockery."

"Oh?" I asked, raising my eyebrows in a mock surprise. "Then why did you come here?"

"To collect the ship. Our commander has ordered us to fetch it."

"He has absolutely no legal standing to give such an order."

"That does not concern me. As far as I know, the ship is Spanish. Where is she?"

"In a very safe place."

This really got the Spaniard's goat.

"Where is it? Damn it!"

I laughed him in the face and said nothing. The Spaniard seemed close to exploding for a moment but checked himself, seeing several of my men moving behind his back.

"If this is all you had been ordered to impart to me, *señor*," I said to him very slowly," then a very good evening to you. I wish you a safe return to your camp. It will be dark soon, and you should bear in mind that our forest can be very treacherous at night. Men have been known to lose their way within it and to disappear without a trace. It is best not to linger after dark. Please be so kind as to convey to the illustrious Don Esteban that I shall call on him tomorrow to pay my respects."

The Spaniard mumbled some sort of reply, and he and his men walked off, this time in the direction of Serima.

"And, oh, *señor*!" I called out after him from afar. "Do remember what I said about the dangers of entering this clearing after dark! We would not want anyone to be hurt accidentally."

Our people, who mostly understood Spanish, had enjoyed our exchange and now joked about it.

The sun had set, and the darkness was thickening. No one from Serima bothered us. I selected Vagura and three fit warriors, and the seven of us—with Aripai, Katawi, and me, set off briskly into the night. Arnak remained behind in charge of the settlement.

As ours was a night excursion, we had no use for rifles, but in addition to pistols, knives, and clubs, I ordered four bows with a sufficient number of arrows.

"Why do we need the bows?" asked Vagura.

"They will be essential."

"Will we shoot the bows in the dark?"

"No."

"Why then?"

"Can't you guess?"

But Vagura couldn't understand the need for bows on this mission. Delighted by his confused expression, I left him to stew in uncertainty.

How many days had I not walked in the forest! When the familiar smell of the jungle now filled my nostrils, its familiar noises filled my ears, and its wet branches snapped at my body as we followed the narrow path, I felt as if my heart grew and my strength returned. Katawi knew the way well and walked briskly in the lead, and we followed him like ghosts.

After walking for almost two hours, the fisherman let us know that we were approaching the island. The bright surface of the river shone through the coastal bush when suddenly, a figure appeared before us on the path. The stranger cleared his throat, Katawi cleared his throat.

It was his son. His father had commanded him to watch the island. The young man now informed us that nothing had changed in the camp. Only in the afternoon, the guards ordered the prisoners to go out onto the sandy beach to relieve themselves, after which they again drove them into the boat. Everyone's hands remained tied, and to make matters worse, the Chayma tied their legs together, too.

The island, according to Katawi's description, was elongated, about a hundred fathoms long, but not more than eighty paces wide, and ran parallel to the shore, separated from it by a deep water channel, not very wide. It had been formed from a sandy shoal, on which, with the passage of time, miscellaneous vegetation sprang up and even several dozen trees.

The Spaniards set up camp on the narrow channel opposite the river bank facing us and were obscured by the island's vegetation from the view of anyone coming out of the Imataca or up or down the main channel of the Orinoco. They did not kindle fires so as not to betray their location by smoke. There were always two guards: one Spaniard and one Indian. So it was also tonight—Katawi's son had noticed in the evening twilight. While two watched over the prisoners, their colleagues slept in the bow of the second boat.

At first, I had planned to paddle up by way of the narrow channel, cut one or two Warao lose, give them a knife to free the others, and a few clubs so that they could attack and overpower their guards, but unsure of their courage and combat skills, I gave up this plan and decided to do the whole project on our own.

The fisherman had kept his two small boats in the coastal thickets well upriver from the island. We found them and quietly lowered them into the water. I gave my comrades last instructions, and above all, I reminded them that we must act quietly to make sure that neither the Spanish in Serima nor the Spanish on the island should ever guess who had freed the Warao.

"The Spaniards on the island, too, did you say?" whispered Vagura. "You mean... we are going to spare their lives?"

"You know me. You know I do not like to kill people if it is not necessary."

"Well, yes, but in this case, it is necessary!"

"I don't think so! There are only four of them. There are five of us, plus Aripai. We will surprise them by hitting them on the head with clubs. If we happen to smash a head open, well, tough luck. But we don't have to hit so hard as to kill them, just enough to put them out of business."

"And we tie them up?"

"Of course! And wrap their heads to make sure they see nothing. Besides, perhaps they won't even have time to come to before we all leave the island again."

I felt that Vagura still had something in mind. And he did. The bows. The matter of the bows bothered him. He asked about them now.

"You say we will hit them with our clubs?" he asked slyly, with a feigned indifference in his voice.

"Yes, with clubs."

"Not in any other way? Only with clubs?"

"Yes, only with clubs."

"Well, then, you have to admit that we didn't need these stupid bows. And I was right all along. We lugged them for nothing."

He wanted to prove his point.

"You little cockerel!" I poked fun at him. "Would you believe it? You have been wrong all along and still are!"

"So the bows are still necessary?

"Very necessary."

"Not that I can see!"

"Think harder!"

We pushed off. I, Katawi, his son, and one warrior in the first boat, Vagura, and the rest following us in the second.

The current soon took us, and we shot downriver. The little

boats, made of bark, could barely hold the eight of us.

Soon, we saw a darker outline on the water: it was the tip of the island. Taking care to avoid the channel, we kept to the mainstream of the river, and after passing the top of the islet, we landed several dozen fathoms below it, on the side facing the main channel of the river. Katawi assured us that the Spaniards were camped only sixty or seventy paces away from us, and all we had to do was cross the narrow strip of vegetation to arrive at their camp.

Everyone already knew the task assigned to him, so we immediately began to work our way through the vegetation. It wasn't too thick or difficult; being careful, we glided almost noiselessly. Suddenly, the bushes opened before us, and we stood at the edge of a beach. In front of us, there were perhaps fifteen paces of sand and then the waters of the side channel.

We saw the Spanish camp a little downriver: a long black shape lying on the sand, easily guessed to be one of the *itauba* pulled ashore, while the other one was anchored on the water.

"In this *itauba* on land," Katawi breathed to me in a whisper, "are the captives. Can you see the sentry watching over them?"

Yes, I noticed a shape like a person sitting on the edge of the boat. This had to be one of the guards. He sat perfectly motionless. Perhaps he was dozing. But where was the other one?

"You said there were two!" I breathed to Katawi.

"Yes, two!"

"So where is the other one?"

Katawi and his son consulted in whispers, but they couldn't explain the absence of the second sentry.

"Maybe he went to sleep?"

"Are you sure the other two sleep in the other boat?"

"Yes!" breathed Katawi's son. "They sleep at the prow of the boat, and the prow is turned towards us."

"Vagura! You hear?"

"I do!"

Walking on the sand, in the shade of the bushes, we would be able to approach to within twenty paces of the boats, but then, to get to the guard, we would have to cross the sandy beach between us and him. These several steps of open space exposed us to danger. In order to reduce it and, at the same time, sniff out where the second sentry was, I decided to use a trick I had learned in the Virginia woods, namely, to raise a false alarm. Larger and smaller stones lay here and there in the sand. So, having instructed Katawi and his son how and when they were to throw them into the water, I went into action.

It was so dark that it was possible for us to sneak along the edge of the thicket without entering it. We trod carefully so that the sand would not crunch under our feet. Moving with excruciating slowness, we eventually got to the place directly in front of the boat with the prisoners. Here, I stopped with one of our men. Kokui was the biggest and strongest beast in our clan. Vagura and his three companions passed us and crept up ahead another dozen steps to get as close to the second *itauba* as possible.

Katawi had not been idle. Far ahead, in the middle of the channel, suddenly water began to splash—those were the stones Katawi and his son threw in the river. The sentry on the *itauba* shuddered: he *had* been dozing! A second and the third stone fell with a splash even louder than the first.

It sounded very strange—as if a large beast were frolicking in the water.

At last! The sentry gave a sign of life. He rose and stretched himself. The strange commotion in the water aroused his curiosity. He walked a few steps along the beach and appeared to stare into the darkness. And when he heard new splashes, he called out in a hushed voice:

"*Señor* Fernando! *Señor* Fernando!"

A man, invisible to us because he had been lying on the sand near the boat, awoke from sleep.

"*Que cosa*? What the devil?" he asked in a sleepy voice.

So here we had them: the Spaniard and the Chayma on guard.

I nudged Kokui and gestured to him that he should take the

Indian while I took care of the Spaniard.

And we jumped. A few light leaps across the sand. There were more splashes in the channel, and the frogs and crickets were making a lot of noise—we got to the boat unnoticed. Our maces descended on the two heads almost simultaneously, wham-bam! The men fell to the ground without feeling. The Spaniard only managed a stifled grunt. The echo of the clubs smashing the skulls had been Vagura's sign.

I jumped towards the other boat, but my help was not needed. Our friends had accomplished the deed. The two sleeping men did not even have time to wake: wham-wham-wham!—and they continued to lie in peace. We now quickly dragged all four into the bush and hog-tied them with bast. The Spaniard's shirts made very nice wrappings for their heads.

Cutting the Warao loose took a blink of an eye. When they wanted to talk or shout, we sternly ordered them to be silent. We pushed the two *itauba* onto the water and divided the men into two crews. Luckily, there were plenty of oars. Katawi knew a nearby bay so hidden by overhanging greenery that the devil himself would never find it. We barely managed to push the two *itauba* in, but once we got in, we were perfectly safe. Here, we examined the cargo of the loaded boat in peace and found that it was indeed full of food supplies: corn, *mandioca* root, as well as dried fish, and strips of dried beef. We were pleased with the plentiful loot, which made us independent of the rest of the tribe for a while, but I was even more pleased with the two barrels of gunpowder I found and a generous pouch of lead.

The Warao confirmed our guesses. They had come from Kaiiwa, the home of Oronapi, our ally and friend. The Spaniards had called on him a few days ago to collect tribute. Because he was unable to satisfy their demands, the invaders raided a remote part of Kaiiwa and rounded up all the men they could catch. Immediately after the attack, they herded them onto their boats and left, and because they were well-armed, Oronapi did not dare pursue them.

The captives knew well what awaited them in Angostura and were grateful to us for deliverance, which they expressed repeatedly.

Having allotted a day's rations to the Warao, I ordered them to take the empty *itauba* and paddle like the devil back to Kaiiwa.

"I will not give you the firearms taken from the Spaniards," I said to them at farewell," because you don't know how to use them. But take the bows and maces of the two Indians so that you can defend yourselves on the way. And—Vagura, listen up!—give them those four bows and arrows."

"Ha! Do you think I hadn't guessed it?" my young friend huffed.

"Ho! You brainy beast! You are more sly than I have supposed!" I snorted in acknowledgment.

Meanwhile, the Warao gathered around and whispered among themselves.

"What is going on?" I asked Aripai.

Aripai did not hear what they said, but soon a rather big and, as I guessed from the sound of his voice, young Warao stepped forward and spoke to me boldly:

"White Jaguar! They call me Manduka, and they say that I am brave and a good fighter. You have saved us from slavery and disgrace. Now, the same Spanish that attacked us are with your people in Serima. These Spaniards will attack your people, I am sure of it. And we owe you help. I don't want to return to Kaiiwa now. I want to stay here and fight the Spanish. Give me a weapon and tell me what to do. I'm coming with you."

"And I!... And I!..." volunteered several others.

Surprised and—I have to admit—very pleased, I looked inquiringly at Vagura:

"Do we take them?"

"And why not?"

"And what about weapons?"

"We will find some bows and maces for them."

"Very well, then," I said to Manduka. "I gladly accept your help. How many of you are there?"

There were eleven. All were eager to take revenge on the

Spaniards.

"Fine," I said. "I welcome you, but on one condition: that you solemnly promise to follow all my orders. Aripai will explain them to you."

As soon as the rest of the Warao had left, we set off on our way back, with the exception of one of our warriors, whom we left with the young fisherman to guard the supply boat.

The complete success of the night expedition—everything had gone to plan since even the opponents never learned who had overcome them—put us in an excellent mood, and when, about midnight, we reached our huts, we were exuberant. Arnak was up, waiting for us, and immediately saw our satisfaction.

"We bring allies!" boasted Vagura. "Eleven Warao want to fight the Spanish!"

"Is this true?" Arnak turned to me.

"Yes," I replied. "They're waiting at the edge of the forest. Take care of them! Find them some huts to sleep in, but make sure as few people see them as possible; at dawn, give them weapons: bows, maces, spears, whatever we got, just no firearms."

Later, as Vagura narrated the course of our night expedition, Arnak suddenly became worried:

"You abandoned those four in the thicket? All tied up? Aren't they going to die?"

"Well, unless some predator gets to them, the Spaniards will find them when they return to the island."

Another devoted soul besides Arnak had been up, waiting for us: Lasana. She brought from her hut a warm meal of boiled fruit palm *buriti*. I hugged her with contentment.

The Four Shots

I slept the calm, profound sleep of the just. But at daybreak, I began to have a nightmare. It suffocated me, and I felt as if an inner voice of my nature was warning me, not allowing me to sleep through a moment of danger. A new day was rising, and it was going to be a day of difficult decisions and of a test of wits and strength against a dangerous enemy. On such a day, who dared to sleep peacefully?

But it was not the nightmare that woke me, but a voice calling to me:

"White Jaguar! White Jaguar!"

Opening my eyes, I saw Aripai leaning over me. Instantly, I became wide awake.

"Aripai! It's you! What happened?"

"Something bad, master!"

I realized immediately that things must have gone very badly indeed: yesterday, he had spoken to me in a familiar way; this morning, I was his "master."

"What happened, my friend?" I asked him.

"Betrayal, sir," he whispered. "Betrayal! I ran away from Serima!"

"What?" I became alarmed. "Has anyone found out where you were last night?"

"No! No! It's Coneso. He's going to betray us!"

"Coneso? Pox on Coneso! What did he do?"

"Nothing, yet! But he's planning to give us to the Spanish."

"You? Which you? Who—you?"

"Everyone who'd been planning to leave Serima with you. You know, after the death of Kanaholo."

"Is Carapana in on this?"

"I don't know, master! But you must defend us! We don't want to go into Spanish service!"

"Yes, of course, Aripai! You stay here with us. Do not go back to Serima. How many people does Coneso want to give to the Spanish, do you know?"

"Many, White Jaguar! Many! All who are not loyal to him. I've heard five times ten, maybe more."

"Whole families?"

"No, just men. The Spanish don't want any women."

"Have they taken any people yet?"

"Many have taken their families and run off into the forest at night. Several families have fled here to you. My woman and her kids are here. But not everyone managed to get away. Those who did not run away last night have been herded together by the Chayma. And Coneso's men are helping the Chayma."

"Coneso's men? On his orders?"

"Coneso has not made any announcement. Still, we all know what they are going to do!"

"And these captives... do they know what is going to happen to them?"

"Oh, yes."

"And they don't resist?"

Aripai looked at me with hesitation.

"There are so many of them, master! Twelve Spaniards with matchlocks. And the Chayma. And Coneso's men. How can anyone resist?"

"Are Coneso's people all such traitors? Will they surrender their own brothers to the Spanish?"

"Whether all, I do not know. But if they can buy their freedom by selling us? Everyone's looking out for his own skin!"

Those were sad words to hear. They were filled with shame and self-doubt. An ugly abyss opened before me. The Arawaks weren't wicked or cowards. My clan had proven this repeatedly. They despised betrayal. One could trust them. So if Coneso's people were capable of such abomination, if they were prepared to buy their own freedom with the slavery of their closest compatriots, then undoubtedly their depraved elders were to blame. The wretched and weak Coneso, the criminal madman Carapana, the malicious Pirokai, brother of Manauri—their example and influence corrupted everyone and everything around them. And they had been rightly afraid of our rejoining the tribe. Rightly so, I thought with rising anger.

Arnak and Vagura entered the hut and confirmed Aripai's words: Coneso was going to hand over his own people to the Spanish.

"But in a year, the Spanish will be back again!" I was getting very angry. "And will take more!"

Aripai shrugged:

"There is no helping that."

"And what do you think, Aripai? What will happen if we stand and fight?"

The Indian's eyes glowed:

"You will defeat them, master! White Jaguar is invincible!"

"That's not what I meant!" I explained. "We will defeat them, for sure. But what will happen then? Will the people selected by Conseo to go into Spanish captivity— will they take up arms and fight alongside us?"

"I think they will fight," said Aripai.

"And you," I turned to my friends. "What do you think about it?"

"If they are not disarmed and we move, then they will probably fight," said Arnak.

"Yes, as long as they have weapons!" said Vagura.

"Have they not yet been disarmed?" I asked. "What news from Manauri? Has his messenger come?"

Just then, the messenger arrived. He had barely managed to get away from Serima: Coneso's men had tried to stop him. He confirmed Aripai's words. We needed to act fast.

"Where are the Warao?"

"We armed them, and they are in Miguel's hut, awaiting orders."

"Very well, let them wait a little longer. What about our men? Are they ready?"

"They're all here."

We left the hut. Everyone was assembled there. Their faces were determined, their eyes fearless, their jaws locked, their postures bold. They were armed like for a military expedition, not just muskets and pistols, but also bows, clubs, and spears. My brave detachment presented itself magnificently. It inspired trust and commanded respect. I must have had a pleased expression at their sight, for the warriors, seeing me, beamed. But, by God, how few of us were there! A handful!

"Sweet Jesus, is this all of us?" I asked Arnak.

"All," replied the boy, and guessing my unease, explained: "Five of us, the Africans, are on the schooner..."

I regretted now that I had sent them all away. Two would have been enough.

"Shall we call them back?"

"But whom do we send to fetch them?"

"Arasibo."

"No. We need Arasibo here. He knows how to shoot a gun."

"Aripai?"

"Very well, we will send Aripai! Bring Miguel back and two more with him!"

"Manauri is in Serima," enumerated further Arnak. "One is with the *itauba* at the mouth of the Imataca. Two had left us for Coneso's faction. There were twenty-one of us on the schooner, twenty-one plus you. Here are twelve. You have ten here, Vagura is the eleventh, and I am the twelfth... Shall we send a messenger to Manauri?"

"No, we will need him here!"

Twelve! Plus me—thirteen, and what a force against us!

Twelve Spaniards, armed to the teeth and aggressive, fifty Chayma under their command. And the tribe was divided, quarreling, brother ready to jump to his brother's throat. How do we defend ourselves against such a fierce enemy?

As I thought these unpleasant thoughts, anger swelled up

inside me against the chief and the sorcerer. The fools had declared war against me, strewn my paths with serpents, and having incapacitated me for days, neglected the most important business of the tribe. Somewhere to the south, an Akawaio war was said to be brewing, and the Spanish invasion was enough to expose the fragility of our defenses.

"Arnak," I asked my friend. "How many spare firearms do we have?"

"Almost thirty long guns and twenty pistols."

"If we ever get through this business with the Spanish, which is not all that certain, we will have to train a larger contingent of warriors."

"These are all the men of our clan!"

"Yes. But we have friends in Serima. We will invite them to join our clan. The hell with what Coneso thinks. And now let's go and see if the beast is as dangerous as they paint him."

Before we left, I bathed in the river, shaved, had my hair trimmed. I ate breakfast and then, with the help of Lasana, donned my Spanish uniform. I did not complain about the thickness of the material or the heaviness of the boots: proper appearance required them.

Supposedly, I looked magnificent.

"Yes!" my friends said, smacking their lips, and Lasana's eyes watered with delight.

"You are too easily impressed!" I pretended to scold her.

"Oh, Yan, you look gorgeous!" Lasana burst out laughing. "You have never yet looked so proud and so handsome! Oh, those poor girls in Serima!"

"Poor girls? Do I look that ravishing?"

"Oh, yes! They will all lose their minds!"

"I would prefer it if the Spaniards lost their minds and left."

I summoned Arnak, Vagura, Arasibo, Kokui, and Lasana to my hut to give them my last confidential instructions:

"We have very few men, and the Spaniards and their allies are

Dancing Arawaks
Arnoldus Montanus, *De Nieuwe en Onbekende Weereld,*
Amsterdam, 1671, Jacon Meurs

a horde. We must trick them into thinking that there are a lot more of us. We have enough spare weapons. So you, Arasibo, and you, Kokui, will take six muskets each, and you, Lasana, will take three fowlingpieces, they are lighter. You will load them with powder only, and each of you will position yourself at the edge of the forest near Serima. Each

of you will stand separately. Stand a good distance away from one another.

"At a sign I give you, you will each fire off all your guns, as fast as you can, one after the other, to make the Spaniards think that the whole forest is crawling with armed men. As soon as you have done this, each of you will grab your guns and run to another place in the forest, load your guns, and await another signal. But the second time, you will load your gun with shot."

"And we?" interjected Vagura. "What shall Arnak and I do?"

"All the rest of you will come with me to Serima as my retinue."

Having agreed signs, we all set off to our tasks.

It was extremely humid and stuffy. The sky was covered with a burning white haze. The sun didn't pierce it, but from that haze, heat belched at us as if from a furnace. As I entered the grove that separated our clearing from Serima, I glanced back at our huts. In recent weeks, they had become as dear to me as my homeland had once been. I resolved I would not allow their peace and happiness to be destroyed by hateful intruders.

Having reached the end of the forest, I assigned a post to Lasana and sent Arasibo and Kokui to find their own spots. They were to wait at the edge of the forest, too, only Arasibo five hundred paces away and Kokui a thousand so that the three of them would surround Serima almost in a semicircle.

I admired Lasana's calm and presence of mind. She was as composed as an experienced warrior. I read in her eyes the immeasurable trust she put in me. At farewell, I gathered her hair with my left hand and gave it a little pull.

"I will not fail you, Charming Palm!" I smiled

"I know," she replied seriously. "I know."

Did I promise the impossible?

Bad things were happening in Serima. We all saw it from a distance. The Spaniards and their Indians, arms in hand, were running among the huts. The shouting of men, crying of children, and wailing of women mingled with harsh orders shouted in Spanish. Among all that chaos, it was hard to make any sense of the situation, and only after we had traveled halfway to the main square did we understand the meaning of the confusion. The invaders were rounding up certain people and driving them to the central square of Serima. The other Arawaks watched the violence impassively, doing nothing to protect the captives.

The dance had begun.

I looked back at my warriors with a bitter smile. "My friends! If any of you don't fancy being in a fight this morning, let him retreat to the woods and help Lasana with her guns! But if you do, do it now because things are going to get very hot very quickly."

"What's the use of talking, White Jaguar?" grunted Arnak.

"We can take the heat," said someone else sharply.

"We wasted the Spanish twice, why not three times?" said someone else. "Just lead us. We'll be fine."

"You little cockerels! Very well, just remember: stay calm, and keep an eye on everything, and watch everything I do."

As soon as we were sighted from Serima, the screaming and running around all died down, and everyone froze. All eyes turned towards us. Even the Spaniards froze and stared at us in silence. In the eery calm that now fell over the settlement, the excitement of several hundred souls was so thick, so palpable, you could cut it with a knife.

Ignoring their surprise, we continued on with slow, careless tread. In the center of the village, under a vast *toldo*—a roof without walls, under which several weeks ago Coneso welcomed us to Serima— stood the elders of the tribe and, with them, the commander of the

Spanish.

We headed in their direction.

A bow shot from the *toldo*, I signaled for Vagura and nine of the men to stop and keep an eye on the group of elders, the square, and the whole riverbank. Meanwhile, Arnak and another fellow followed me, each to one side, covering my back.

When we approached to within a dozen paces of the *toldo*, the Spanish commander stepped forward and, taking off his hat to me and lowering it to the ground in a gesture of respect, called to me from afar:

"Allow me, illustrious *caballero*, to express my boundless admiration to you: a guest in our country who had bravely penetrated this inhuman wasteland and whose extraordinary and alarming fame precedes him!"

Such unexpectedly polite words, uttered in a warm tone, surprised me so much that for a moment, I forgot what I was going to say. But quickly regaining my composure, I took off my hat, swept the ground with it as energetically as the Spaniard had done, and said:

"Please accept my expressions of profound respect and esteem, *señor*. It gives me indescribable pleasure to meet such a refined and cultured gentleman as yourself in these parts. Allow me also to take this opportunity to clarify that I find myself in your country by accident rather than of my own free will and that whatever fame may have attached to my person has done so against my personal inclinations. I am a man of peace."

I said this in my Spanish, which was probably less smooth than I record it here, but Don Esteban understood me perfectly, for he answered immediately:

"I have heard of your exploits, *caballero*, and I know that it was not your fault that your paths and those of the Spanish have twice crossed under less than amicable circumstances and have had regrettable consequences. Our mutual friend, Pedro Martinez, has told me all about it."

With such politeness, we approached each other and shook hands. The Spaniard must have been thirty-five. His face exuded kindness, and especially his mouth, shaping into the most charming of smiles. But when I studied his face more closely, I was astonished to see his eyes: they were cold and took no part in the polite exchange at all. Indeed, they seemed to belong to another man, were strangely icy, and had a striking expression of severity. The eyes said something different than the mouth, but which expressed the man's true feeling?

I trembled at the realization that only a moment ago, I was so recklessly inclined to trust beautiful appearances, taking the smiling lips and kind words at face value.

"A wolf in sheep's clothing!" I thought to myself. "A wolf! And his wolfish nature is showing in his eyes."

"By my honor, *caballero*, I awaited your grace as a bride awaits her bridegroom," continued the Spaniard, smiling and taking me by the arm in a friendly way. "Because I need your help, and without it, I can't advance a step in my business. This Coneso is a dishonest scoundrel, a disgusting swindler, and a lousy dog! Surely, Don Juan, you must agree with me."

"Entirely."

"Ha! I knew all along that your grace and I would come to an understanding in an instant!"

"I am ever and always for peace and understanding," I said. "But what understanding might your grace possibly have in mind?" I asked innocently, raising my eyebrows slightly.

"Coneso and his men do not wish to live up to the promises they had made me. They think to short-change me and send me away with nothing! Not only do they not intend to repay the debts they had contracted, but, what is worse, immersed in ignorance as they are, they do not see the great favor that we wish to bestow upon them. Ungrateful wretches, they resist me over everything."

"How could that be, your grace? They do not wish to accept your favor?"

"Would your grace believe it? The tribe is to nominate fifty young men to go to Angostura to learn how to cultivate land more fruitfully and become brave and successful farmers. After two years, they will return here and, working more productively for themselves and the tribe, multiply everyone's abundance, happiness, and well-being."

How beautiful this sounded in the mouth of the Spaniard and how different it looked in reality! I had had an opportunity to learn from my Arawak friends what this "fruitful work on Spanish haciendas" looked like. As did the rest of our tribe—and they were not going to be fooled by such pretty talk.

"Fifty young men? Fifty?" I whistled in astonishment. "By God, surely, when they return here, they will make this tribe the most exemplary and the happiest tribe in Venezuela!"

The Spaniard studied my face carefully, but finding nothing untoward, he smiled—with his eyes. Yes. For the first time since I laid my eyes on him, his pupils came to life. Only it was a rather unusual smile of the eyes, a little haughty and a little mocking. It was obvious that Don Esteban had not sensed my irony.

"How very true, *caballero*!" he agreed with me in a slightly overindulgent manner, as one does when speaking to a well-disposed but not very intelligent child. "But that's not quite the whole truth! For while these Arawaks will indeed become a more modern and happier tribe after the return of the fifty; yet, here, in Venezuela, we have many other even happier tribes that have already attained even higher levels of cultural advancement."

"Oh, how fortunate those tribes must be!" I exclaimed.

At this, the Spaniard became slightly confused, for I may have exclaimed a little louder than true admiration warranted. But after a moment's hesitation, he seemed to attribute my strange words and tone of voice to my generally poor command of the Spanish language.

Then, pointing to the surrounding countryside with an expansive gesture, Don Esteban said:

"I know, *caballero*, that you have been here only a short while. But I know also that you have a great influence among these Arawaks. Not all, perhaps, but some: you do have your following and are their unquestioned leader."

Here, he glanced briefly at my squad, holding nonchalantly their guns at the ready.

"Now, Coneso suggested to me that I take *your* Indians and *your* Negroes to Angostura, but I don't want to do that. First, because your people have just arrived, are exhausted with travel, and deserve a rest. And, second, neither you nor your people owe me any debt, unlike Coneso, who does. But, you see, Coneso, the dog, now says that he has no people. That those whom he had planned to give me ran away to the forest at night! I do know that some people fled into the forest last night, but many still remain. Therefore, I beg you, sir, to persuade the distrustful that it is in their best interest, and in the best interest of the tribe, to go to Angostura. And please make Coneso understand that if he doesn't give me the full fifty he owes me, I will skin him alive."

"And these people? Who are they?" I asked, pointing to the group of captives standing nearby under Chayma guard. "What are they waiting for?"

"They will go with us. But there are just twenty-three of them, and I am to have fifty."

"They look rather gloomy to me."

"Because they are uninformed! They don't know what awaits them!"

"Or maybe they know only too well?"

I said it slowly, seemingly indifferently, but Don Esteban fixed his stare on me, again watchful and unspeakably cool.

He came quite close to me. He had black, bushy eyebrows and long, dark eyelashes, but his irises were not black but grey like lead, which gave his eyes that hard, steely look. Now, even his lips had grown cold and hardened with marked sternness.

"*Señor caballero!*" he said slowly, stressing every word. He stood so close to me that I could feel his breath on my face. "*Señor caballero,* I hope that your grace has heard and understood the meaning of what I have just told him."

"I am not exactly certain which part of your fine speech you are alluding to, *señor*. Be so kind as to remind me."

"I have assured your grace that I will not touch any of your men."

"Ah, yes. Thank you most profusely, Don Esteban."

"But I did this in the hope that, in your own interest, you might help me fetch the fifty men I need from among Coneso's men."

"And if, like these Arawaks over there," I pointed to the captives, "I should fail to understand my best interest, will I be offending your grace?"

"Now, it is my turn not to understand. Would your grace speak more clearly?"

"What should happen, *caballero*, if I should refuse to assist you?"

Don Esteban squinted his eyes as if aiming at me with an invisible matchlock.

"Do not imagine, *caballero*, that I haven't noticed the note of irony with which you have been kind to grace your speech a little earlier. However, now you are clearly mocking me. Let us cast mockery aside! For if your grace does not assist me in my task, it may very well happen that I should remember Coneso's advice regarding your people's aptitude for agricultural work."

"*Señor caballero*! Certainly, I am mistaken, or is that a threat?"

"As your grace pleases. We could call it a threat."

Putting on an exaggerated display of terror, I shook my head slowly: left, then right, then left, and then—burst out laughing:

"Please forgive my naivete, but a rather entertaining thought has occurred to me. What if my people should run away into the forest just like the others? What then?"

"Do I not have you as hostage?"

"But what if I, too, should run away?"

"I do not believe, your grace, that you will be able to. My people are swift runners and excellent shots."

"Would you permit me to bring to your attention, *señor*, the fact that my people have firearms?"

Don Esteban shrugged his shoulders dismissively:

"Indians! Indians can't shoot!"

"Ah. But maybe some can?"

We were still standing—far too long!—in the same place where we had shaken hands, a dozen or so paces from the *toldo*. And all the while, under its wide roof, sat Coneso on his stool waiting for us to approach, and next to him stood Manauri, serving as an interpreter, and also the chiefs: Pirokai and Fujidi, and behind them, several other principal Indians, all armed. Pedro was there, too, but there was no sign of Carapana.

"Before I answer you, *caballero*," I turned to the Spaniard, speaking now in all seriousness. "Before I give you my binding answer to your request, allow me first to speak to the people who will go to Angostura and then consider the situation."

Don Esteban hesitated for a moment, but seeing my smile and not wanting to appear cowardly, he relented:

"Very well. Go ahead, *señor*."

I called Manauri and asked him in a whisper to give me a brief account of what had happened in the last hour. He confirmed everything I have learned from Aripai and Don Esteban. When he was done, I asked:

"Those twenty-three over there, kept under guard, are they our supporters? Is that why Coneso wants to give them up?"

"Yes, every one of them."

"He didn't give up any of his men?"

"Not one."

"Son of a dog! And those six thugs, standing under arms behind the backs of Prokai and Fujudi, who are they?"

"His guard. Three are sons of Coneso, one is my nephew, son of Pirokai, and two are Fujudi's brothers. All family."

"Keep an eye on them to make sure none shoots us. Now, Manauri, go to Vagura and collect your gun—get one loaded with shot. And then, let's go talk to the prisoners."

"Will Don Estaban allow it?"

"He already has."

"Stupid!"

"No. He's not stupid. But he is overconfident."

"Are we going to fight?"

"I don't know yet. I am hoping we can avoid it."

When Manauri returned, we went, as I had promised, to the group of twenty-three captives. They stood in the middle of the yard, huddled in a pitiful, defenseless mass, guarded on all sides by the Chayma. Those Chayma were a hostile bunch. They were warlike Caribs living on the *llanos* north f of Orinoco. In place of the usual talismans, they wore brass crosses to signify that they were Christians.

The prisoners, seeing me coming towards them, raised their heads and looked lively as if waking from a great stupor. Each pair of eyes suddenly shone with a ray of hope.

"Are you content to go with the Spanish?" I asked them.

The question sounded almost like an insult or a sneer; all responded with a vehement denial.

"If not, then why did you not run away? And why do you not defend yourselves?"

One of the older prisoners, about thirty years old, replied:

"We couldn't, master! They attacked us so suddenly. Others managed to flee, but we haven't."

"Well, I'd like to come to your rescue. But if I start a fight with the Spaniards, will you fight also, or will you just stand around like women and see what develops?"

My words caused quite a commotion. The Chayma guards suddenly became concerned, and a few came up closer, unambiguously brandishing their weapons.

Simultaneously, Arnak whispered to me that a son of Coneso was approaching from the direction of the *toldo*.

"Sent here to spy on us," I observed. "It's better that they don't know what we're talking about here. Jump in front of him, Arnak, and order him away."

"And if he doesn't listen?"

"You figure out a way. Just don't start a fight."

"Look! Some Spaniard is coming, too! Sent by Don Esteban, no doubt."

"That's alright. I am pretty sure he doesn't understand Arawak."

I turned to the captives again.

"If it comes to fighting," said the young man, "we will all do it. We just don't know when and how."

"You will attack your guards!"

"With bare hands?"

"Yes, with bare hands. There will be great confusion. Vagura's people will throw you some maces and spears, but mainly, you will have to count on surprise. Remember that while this goes on, we will be shooting."

"Yes, White Jaguar. We will do it."

"Now choose from amongst yourselves three men, who will be summoned in a moment to the *toldo* to consult with the chief and the Spaniards."

"We will."

"One more thing. Once we get rid of the Spanish, what will you do? Stay in Serima? With Coneso?"

"Never!" several voices cried out. "Coneso sold us! He betrayed us! We will not stay with him."

"Will you go away with our clan?"

"Wherever you say!"

Arnak had not let Coneso's son approach us, and the two men stood quarreling with each other halfway, but now, there was no need for that anymore: we were walking back towards the *toldo*. Before we reached it, a new altercation broke out in the square.

Several Spanish soldiers approached Vagura's men and began to make fun of our warriors. Our Arawaks understood Spanish because of their recent captivity, but they ignored the taunts with exemplary indifference. For the object of particular hilarity, the Spaniards chose our muskets and laughingly expressed their doubt whether the guns were even loaded. At one point, the most brazen Spaniard decided to snatch the musket from Vagura's hands to see if the pan had powder, and he grabbed its barrel. Vagura did not let the musket out of his hands. There was a scuffle.

Seeing that a general fight might easily break out prematurely, I shouted from a distance to Vagura to let go of the musket. The youth immediately obeyed me. Both I and Don Esteban arrived at the site of the scuffle almost at once.

The soldier pulled the cock amidst laughter and expressed exaggerated amazement at seeing any powder at all. With mocking enthusiasm, he held the gun out for other Spaniards, including Don Esteban, to admire the gunpowder.

"*Que miraculo!*" he cried. "It is loaded!"

The clown did not notice that Vagura, with an ominous wrinkle on his forehead, slowly took his bow off his left shoulder, nocked an arrow, and aimed it at the Spaniard. I approached the boy and, with a menacing face, ordered him to lower his bow. Then, I ordered the soldier to return the musket. The brawler didn't like it very much, but Don Esteban gave the order, and he relented.

"Your men do not seem to have much respect for our skill with firearms," I said cheerfully to Don Esteban.

"On my honor, no!" laughed the Spaniard at my joke, but his eyes remained cold as steel.

"Maybe you gentlemen would like to test the skill of my men?"

"And how would we do that? At any rate," Don Esteban waved his hand dismissively, "time flies. Let us move with our business, shall we?"

Looking around, I noticed some fifty paces away, several empty gourd vessels the size of a human head suspended on lianas to dry.

"Why don't we shoot at those things," I pointed to the gourds.

"They're too small!" asserted the Spaniard. "They'll miss!"

"And what if they do not?"

"Very well," Don Esteban did not hide his amusement. "Why don't you, your grace, select your best sharpshooter and let us see what he can do."

"No, not the best," I said. "Not the best, but any. And not one, but three! Your grace can select himself which of my Indians should shoot."

Don Esteban chose them, thinking that he would ridicule both them and me. He chose two men as to whom I knew that they were good shots. About the third, I had my doubts.

"Choose the largest gourd," I whispered to him, but he, as if offended by my advice, looked at me reproachfully.

I stood a little apart with Don Esteban while Vagura gave his men last-minute instructions. He commanded his men well, and despite that, the Spaniards kept cracking jokes about his young age, taunting a baby face who, instead of drinking his mother's milk, reached foolishly for gunpowder.

"Can we shoot now?" asked Vagura.

"Will your grace allow it?" I turned courteously to Don Esteban.

"Very well," he said and clapped his hands. "Fire away!"

The three men stood in a line, their muskets by their legs at the ready. At Vagura's signal, the first man raised his musket, cradled it against his shoulder, aimed briefly, fired, and then the second, and then the third. The first gourd shattered into pieces, of the second, only a small fraction remained, and the third disappeared as completely as the first.

A great weight was lifted off my heart.

Having fired, my men kept their composure and immediately began to load their guns, heedless of the uproar which the Spaniards raised after a moment of stupor. Amazement, disbelief, bewilderment, and even fear were reflected on their bearded faces—the Spaniards were good sportsmen and applauded good shooting. But my squad remained unmoved as if they didn't care. Only Vagura cheerfully flashed his eyes and sent a taunting smirk at the Spaniard who had tried to joke with him. Don Esteban paused, clearly concerned. He avoided direct eye contact as if he wanted to hide from me what went on inside his head.

"All our past victories over the Spaniards we owe entirely to this," I said kindly to him, kindly but stressing every word: "Our opponents did not seem to take us seriously enough."

A brief, sour glance of Don Esteban showed me that he had caught my drift.

"This could have been a lucky accident," he said, referring to our display of sharpshooting.

A small mongrel dog, probably frightened by the gunshots, ran out from among the huts and began to bark. When Vagura saw it, he stepped forward a little, raised his musket up to his eye, aimed, and fired. He did it so quickly that I had not had the chance to stop the hothead. Although the dog was running about and more than forty paces away, it fell as if cut down.

The nearest Spaniard walked up to it and kicked it, then turned towards us.

"*Ay, caramba!*" he exclaimed, staring at Vagura, his eyes full of fearful admiration. "You shot him in the head!"

Don Esteban seemed to become very pensive. He frowned, his face seemed to age suddenly, he stroked his beard with his right hand. Then he turned towards me with a genial smile.

"And how many sharpshooters like these does your grace have?" he asked me, studying me with his cold eyes.

"Alas, too few!" I said. "I have these here, which you see, and a couple dozen others currently in those woods over there."

"In the woods? Over there? Why?"

"Just resting in the shade. It is so hot here in the square. So they're resting and awaiting my orders."

He looked at me curiously.

"Don Juan, You Are the Devil"

As we slowly approached the *toldo*, where Coneso still sat surrounded by his retinue, I turned to Arnak and whispered to him to send a messenger to Lasana, Arasibo, and Kokui: let them do immediately as we had agreed.

Once in the *toldo*, Don Esteban and I sat down opposite the chief on the two stools prepared for us.

"And where is Manauri's stool?" I rebuked Coneso. "Get him a stool immediately!"

The chief did not object and sent a man to his hut to fetch a stool. We waited for his return in silence, facing each other, each with his armed retinue behind his back: behind Don Esteban stood the sergeant who had searched for our schooner the day before and the chief of the Chayma.

Our faces were calm, but we watched each other carefully; we all felt the tension in the air. Coneso's lower lip, full and sensual, now hung like a flaccid tripe, a sad symbol of the dullness of his wit. He had a bad conscience and realized how dangerous the whole situation was for him and his prospects as a chief of the tribe. Don Esteban, by contrast, was restless, waiting to start the talks with barely concealed impatience. I realized that a man in such a state was especially dangerous, prone to sudden anger and violent action. And I was aware that matters had advanced so far that there were only two alternatives: either I would win a decisive diplomatic victory, or we would fight.

When the fourth stool was brought, and Manauri sat down, I addressed him loud enough for all to hear:

"You, Manauri, will translate for Don Esteban as accurately as possible every word which we will now speak here in Arawak. And you," I looked at Coneso and his people, "you will answer me clearly and honestly if you wish to avert a disaster."

Coneso and his men remained gloomily silent. With the permission of Don Esteban, I ordered three representatives of the captives to be present at the council. When they came, they stopped behind me, next to Arnak, as if to emphasize their separation from Coneso.

"We are not all assembled yet," I said. "Coneso! Summon the village people to stand around us."

"Whatever for?" the chief raised a suspicious glance at me. "Surely, we don't need women and children here."

"Let the women and children come, too. I guarantee that no harm will come to them."

Reluctantly, Coneso sent out the summons, and the people began to assemble. They were indeed mostly women and children, though a few fearful men also appeared. When we were surrounded by their crowd, I ordered silence and spoke up, not hiding my anger:

"And where is Carapana, the murderer of Kanaholo?" I asked everyone a question. "Why isn't he here?"

No one spoke.

"Speak! Where is Carapana?"

"He went into the forest," grunted Fujudi. "To perform a magic ritual."

"What?" I showed my outrage. "He performs a ritual while Serima is in danger? Is that how much he cares for his people? You people have a coward, not a sorcerer!"

The people heard me in speechless horror. Carapana was still a formidable force. And Coneso was livid, staring at me with open hatred.

"You Coneso asked me for help," I said, turning to him. "And I will help, but I first demand some answers. These twenty-three men, designated for the Spaniards, who are they? From what lineages do they come?"

"From all lineages," said Coneso. "All except yours."

"Ah, yes. Not from mine. And why have you not delivered fifty, as Don Esteban demands?"

"Others ran away to the forest."

"What do you mean, 'others'? There are plenty of other young men in Serima, able-bodied men whom Don Esteban could use. He could take them.”

“I have not selected them. I have selected the others. They are not good.”

“Not good? Not good? What do you mean, Coneso? Not good for what?”

Coneso’s eyes shone with angry defiance. He replied:

“They are not suitable to remain here.”

“Why don’t you speak honestly, Coneso? *You* want to remove those men from the tribe.”

“Yes. The chief wants to remove them from the tribe,” interjected Pirokai defiantly. “But only for two years!”

“And those who ran away into the forest, are they removed from the tribe, too?”

“Yes, they are. We dedicate them all to Don Esteban.”

“That’s excellent, Coneso!” I called out in a strong voice for all to hear. “Since you, Coneso, renounce your power over these twenty-three and also over those in the forest, I hereby accept them into our clan!”

And then I turned to the three captives present:

“Do you agree?”

“We agree,” said their foreman. “We want to join your lineage.”

Manauri was supposed to translate my words for Don Esteban, but as I went on, he seemed to be experiencing increasing difficulties, and at one point, he stopped translating altogether.

“As soon as I release you,” I continued speaking to the delegation of the captives, “you will go back to your group and inform them of our decision. You will then find those who have run away into the forest and tell them the same. Then all if you will collect your belongings, leave Serima, and move to our settlement.”

“I forbid it!” snorted Coneso, and Pirokai and Fujudi echoed him:

“It is impossible!”

"Have you lost your minds? You have just said for all of us to hear that you remove these people from your tribe. Are you women that you change your mind from moment to moment?"

"I forbid it!" spat Coneso in anger.

I then turned to him and, staring him directly in the face, I began to speak slowly and clearly:

"Shut your stupid mouth, you disgusting wretch! If you are unable to save your own people from slavery, then at least don't drive them into it! Do you know what Don Esteban calls you? He calls you a mangy dog, a dishonest scoundrel, and a dishonorable swindler! And every honest man has the right to call you that, every man in this tribe. What kind of a chief gives up his own people into bondage without putting up a fight? What kind of chief divides his own people into good and bad?"

"This is not true!" snorted Coneso.

"The men you reject, the men you sacrifice to the Spanish— how are they worse than the others? I will tell you how: they do not want to live under a sorcerer who is a murderer and a chief who is a coward!"

My words seemed to paralyze Coneso and render him speechless.

"Why don't you send your own three sons into slavery, Coneso? Or send Pirocai's son? Or send the two brothers of Fujudi? Are they any better than others? No, they are not. But you do not send them away because they are willing to accept a mangy dog like you for a chief!"

As I was still speaking, a shot rang out in the forest. The atmosphere was so tense that everyone jumped at the sound. A menacing echo rolled over Serima, but before it died out, a second shot rang out, followed by a third, fourth, fifth. Some shots rang out together. It was hard to count how many there were.

"What this?!" exclaimed stunned Don Esteban, jumping up. "Is this an attack? Have you ordered your men to shoot?"

"No, Don Esteban! No! This is not an attack," I explained to him in Spanish. "My men are practicing in the forest. Maybe they are sending a warning to Coneso, too. Coneso is not a popular chief, and I think my men are angry at him. But this is not against you. You are an honored guest in our village. As long as you are here, you are under my protection. No one will dare attack you or any of your men without my permission."

The Spaniard, standing up, gazed across the village and, seeing Vagura's men standing at ease, albeit guns in hand, he relaxed a bit.

"But your men are here," he said.

"Some of my men are here, that's true," I corrected him. "Over there, in the forest, there are more. They are angry at Coneso, but they mean you no harm."

I returned to my conversation with the elders:

"Your miserable chief has failed to protect his tribe. But I will not fail you. I assure you that none of these twenty-three will go with the Spaniards. Moreover, I promise you that no one will go with the Spanish without a fight. I promise you that, and I will keep my promise."

More gunshots resounded, though in another part of the forest. Don Esteban stared at me, clearly shaken.

"Your grace, pay no attention to that racket. This is my people again reminding Coneso not to do anything foolish. You and your people are safe."

"What is this this firing? Who is firing and why?"

"It is all my men, Don Esteban. They are stationed in various places throughout the forest. They watch Serima and guard all approaches."

"Please tell me immediately what you have said to the Indians!" the Spaniard shouted at me. "Your man has stopped translating! What have you been saying to them?"

"As you can guess, your grace, I have told them things they were not pleased to hear."

Another round of shots rang out in the forest, yet in another location. Don Esteban, who had hitherto considered himself the master of the situation on account of his Spaniards and his Chayma, sensed that the ground was shifting under his feet.

"Thirteen shots," said his sergeant when the shooting stopped. "Thirteen guns."

"No!" shook his head the chief of the Chayma. "Nine!"

They were both wrong: Arasibo had only seven guns.

And as he still spoke, more guns shots came from yet another part of the forest. This was the work of Kokui.

"Ten thousand devils!" yelled the sergeant and ran into the square. Like a lunatic, he began to yell at the top of his voice, summoning both the Spaniards and the Chayma to himself and placing them in defensive positions. We looked at him as if he had gone crazy.

I turned to Don Esteban:

"Why is your man running around like that? If he pulls your guards, your captives will scatter."

I watched Don Esteban carefully.

He was clearly very close to an explosion: his eyes grew dark, he seemed half-conscious. Huge pearls of sweat appeared on his forehead and flowed down his face.

"What is this?" he boomed again in a mixture of anger and fear.

"I will explain it to you right now!" I said and turned to Manauri:

"Please translate into Arawak everything I say in Spanish."

And then I said to Don Esteban:

"*Caballero*! You have asked what these shots in the forest mean. I shall now have the honor of explaining it to you, but first, I most humbly beg of you not to jump to quick and ill-considered judgment of the matter. I beg of you to think and act as you have so far: calmly and rationally. Since both you and I are honorable and rational men, I foresee no difficulty, but please bear in mind that the situation is touchy, and any rash conduct may lead to regrettable consequences.

"Well, then. First of all, I have just relieved Chief Coneso of command over the men he had consigned to you."

Don Esteban seemed to misinterpret my words in the way in which I had hoped he would, for he seemed to settle back in his stool with relief.

"Secondly, Don Esteban, I have the honor to inform you that I shall not allow any man of this tribe, not now and not ever, to go into service in Angostura."

"What?" his arteries swelled at his neck and his temples, and his eyes nearly popped out of his head. He quickly reached into his belt where his pistol was.

"By God," I said softly. "Do not be angry, *señor*! Look behind my back, please!"

He looked—and this helped take the tension down a notch, for he found himself staring into the barrel of Arnak's blunderbuss.

"I have already told you, *señor*, that I have had to kill your compatriots twice, both times because they underestimated my strength and my determination to stand by my principles. Let us make sure this does not happen for the third time today."

My calm confidence seemed to calm him down. Scales fell off his eyes. He looked at me as if he wanted to poison me with his gaze.

"Your deputy is a brave man," I continued, "but he is clearly inclined to act hastily. Please advise him to stop doing whatever he is doing. We must resolve this little disagreement like civilized men and without unnecessary loss of life."

Don Esteban obeyed, gnashing his teeth, and issued the necessary order to his deputy. When the first moment of shock passed, he appeared to recover his composure and to look around more calmly to evaluate the situation.

"What does your grace propose?" he asked me suddenly.

"Peace and alliance."

His eyes flashed like daggers.

"Your grace, you are mocking me!"

"God forbid I ever should!"

"Surely, you would not attack us unprovoked."

"Certainly not. I will only shoot you in self-defense."

"You do realize my men can also shoot?"

"Who would ever dare doubt it?" I expressed my appreciation with a polite bow. "But what use is that against overwhelming odds? And I assure you, Don Esteban, that if it does come to shooting, we will bitterly regret not being able to grant you the opportunity to say a *Pater Noster*[7] before you meet Your Maker."

There was a moment of deafening silence. Don Esteban appeared to accept that my words were spoken in earnest. He subdued the emotions raging in his heart and the anger he could not unleash on anyone. From his frozen face covered with deathly pallor, he gazed at me with eyes that, for the first time since we met, expressed something other than predatory calculation: a kind of reluctant admiration.

"Don Juan!" he murmured. "You are the devil incarnate. But do not think you can get away with killing a Spaniard this time! Do not forget in whose name we are here."

"I do not, Don Esteban. I know who the *corregidor* of Angostura is, and I am not confusing him with the Almighty. I believe you may be overestimating the power you serve."

"*Señor*! You are in Venezuela, on the property of His Majesty Philip the Fifth!"

"No, Don Esteban. I am not in Venezuela. I am on the edge of an infinite wilderness where no white man has ever held power of any kind. And surely, the way you conduct yourself with respect to these Indians does not indicate that you consider them subjects of your noble and benevolent king. I believe you treat them as enemies in an enemy country."

Then, slowly, I rose from my stool, walked up to the Spaniard, and looking him in the eye, I said emphatically:

"Enough of this idle talk! Let us talk like *gente de razon*—reasonable men—among which I count us both. I beg you, *señor*, more

---

[7] "Our father." A prayer.

sense and less conceit! I did not speak of peace and alliance in vain. We have common interests and common enemies. You just have to look a little further than the end of your own nose to see it. Do you really have Venezuela's best interests at heart? If so, that is good! Accept, therefore, what I truthfully tell you: I intend to serve your country and your king, along with these Indians. I intend to defend your borders if only the pigheadedness of your superiors does not prevent me from doing so."

And I told him everything I knew about the Akawaio and their projected expedition into the lower Orinoco valley, the rumor of which had already reached Don Esteban's ears. He was also no stranger to the reports that the Akawaio were preparing the invasion not of their own accord but at the urging of the Dutch factories in the Essequibo Basin. However, only when I revealed to Don Esteban my suspicions about the expedition—namely that it was perhaps not just an ordinary slave raid on the native population but—who knows?— perhaps the beginning of a larger push by the Dutch into the Orinoco, and therefore, into the territory of Venezuela—that the Spaniard's eyes shone with a new light. He understood. He understood because past history had taught him that the Dutch, the English, and the French had all, at various times, invaded parts of the Spanish New Granada and taken possession of them. And now, who could vouch that the Dutch were not planning to move into the Orinoco as well?

"And if the Akawaio, the mercenaries of the Dutch, should come," I summed up my position for the Spaniard, "then we will defend this country and, therefore, the whole of Venezuela. But how can we defend it when you, Spaniards, you want to weaken us by taking fifty of our best warriors as slaves?"

"It is true, indeed, *señor*," Don Esteban agreed, suddenly grinning a friendly grin. "Your argument is reasonable, and I accept it."

Whether he agreed with me so completely, I had grave doubts. I guessed rather that, faced with being forced to accept a humiliating climb-down from his original demand for fifty slaves, he preferred to pretend a mutually beneficial alliance: the pretense of a reasonable compromise as opposed to total defeat. Glad to find a solution that allowed him to retreat without loss of dignity, he began to nod agreement with a pretended enthusiasm, to smile sweetly, and to slap his knee with his hand in a display of contentment.

"We are, therefore, your grace, your allies," I said.

Then, suddenly, loud screams interrupted my words.

They came from far away, from the direction of the forest. It was hard to figure out at first who was yelling and why, though the words sounded Spanish. The voice approached quickly as if the man were rushing towards us. We all stood up.

"Some Spaniard," said Arnak, who stepped a little aside to see better.

"Alone?" I asked.

"Alone."

"Unarmed?"

"Unarmed."

Reassured, I sat down again on my stool, curious to see what further developments might bring. From the first, I had had a hunch that I knew what this screaming was about, but when I saw the messenger in his torn shirt, his eyes opened wide with fear, and when Don Esteban, upon seeing him, shouted, "Fernando!" in surprise, I knew for certain: this was the Spaniard whom I had clubbed the night before on the island on the Orinoco.

"A catastrophe!" the runner cried, gasping for air. "Defeat! Desperation! Misfortune!"

"Talk sense!" boomed Don Esteban at him.

"The captives have escaped!" groaned Fernando.

"Escaped? No! How could they have escaped?"

"They escaped! Ghosts helped them! Oh, divine retribution!"

"What ghosts? Stop this nonsense! Have you lost your mind?"

"But they escaped!"

"All of them?"

"All, *señor*!"

"Where to?"

"We don't know! They took both boats!"

"They took the boats?!" exclaimed Don Esteban in such a voice as if he were at the end of his tether. "You've been sleeping, you bastards, instead of watching!"

"I swear before God! I was not sleeping! I was watching!"

"*Señor corregidor* will break your bones when he hears about that! How did this happen?"

"We don't know ourselves! In the dark, out of the blue, we all got a blow on the head and passed out! When we came to, we were lying in the bush hog-tied! We managed to free ourselves eventually, but the Warao and the boats were gone. It was the evil spirits who did it, sire! Some unclean force!"

"You idiot!" growled Don Esteban and threw a long, eloquent look at me. "I know who those ghosts are!"

Fernando, panting, speaking in a trembling, confused voice, kept turning around and looking back towards the forest, from where he had arrived, until at last exploded:

"And... *Señor comandante!* The forest is crawling with Indians! They chased me! They have guns!"

"They shot at you?"

"I don't know. But they had guns!"

"How many?"

"The whole forest is swarming with them!"

Don Esteban turned pale, bit his lip, and he stared grimly ahead. Clearly, unpleasant thoughts ran through his mind.

I decided that the best policy was to press the point.

"Given the threat hanging over us," I resumed where I had left off a moment ago, "I think we have no choice but to enter into an alliance, the Spanish crown and us Indians."

I said it without changing my tone of voice or expression of my face as if there had been no incident with Fernando.

"And to this end, I require that both you, *señor*, and the illustrious *corregidor* of Angostura, in your own interest, recognize my authority over the Arawak and the Warao of this area.”

“And the Warao?” asked Don Esteban, raising his eyebrows.

“And the Warao! We—the Arawak and the Warao—have entered into a solemn covenant by which each nation will come to the aid of the other. And therefore, whoever attacks the Warao becomes our enemy, regardless of who he is. The Akawoi, the Dutch, or—whoever.”

I put special emphasis on the last word.

“And if the *corregidor* does not agree?” snarled Don Esteban with bile.

“Then I will rule this forest without his consent,” I said simply. “And I assure you, *caballero*, you and your *corregidor*, that whether you like it or not, all the settlements of the Warao and of the northern Arawaks are now under the protection of my men.”

A murmur went through the assembled Indians. They knew by now that I never spoke idle words, and they had just watched me deal successfully with Don Esteban. I could see that they welcomed my words, and even the elders seemed to glance at me in a friendlier manner, though they looked to Don Esteban to see whether the Spaniard might not explode in fury.

But nothing of the sort happened. He did show his teeth, yes, but—in a broad smile. He stood up and reached out to me with his hand. We shook.

“What the *corregidor* thinks and decides,” exclaimed the Spaniard eagerly, “I cannot guarantee, *caballero*. But for my part, I accept your authority over these two tribes. Don Juan! I repeat, you are the devil incarnate! And if so, then it is not good to have you as an enemy. Let us make a friendly alliance between us. You defend yourself against the Akawoi, and may God be with you. I take God for my witness that I no longer require anything from you.”

And hugging me, he looked into my eyes, radiant with kindness flowing from his smiling mouth, but his gaze remained as it ever was, inscrutable and freezing to the marrow.

“The devil take him!” I thought to myself. “Behind this smile lurks betrayal. I know it. The devil take that lying face!"

When Manauri translated his words, a great rejoicing arose among the Arawaks. Cheerful cries echoed across the settlement. And one word was repeated more than any other: *Chu-an! Chu-an!*

This was my Spanish name—as Arawaks pronounced it. The word had spread all the way to the forest that fate had turned, that no one would be taken to Angostura, no one would be dragged off by the Spaniards. The twenty-three captives had long since scattered among the settlement and were now gathering their weapons and belongings as quickly as possible and hastily carrying them across the clearing in the direction of our settlement.

Meanwhile, Coneso, pleased with the Spanish climb-down, ordered a feast to honor the Spaniards and my clan, but I refused to drink *kashiri* and ordered my men not to touch it. Dancing and singing began, and again and again, among the singing, we heard: *Chu-an!* And the Serima girls winked at the Spaniards and Chayma Indians.

As the feast went on, Coneso and Fujidi approached me, already a little tipsy, and Coneso said that he would like to give the Spaniards a gift and asked me whether I would let him gift the horse to Don Esteban. I willingly consented, for the horse was of no use to us in the forest and had already begun to grow thin, and merely by looking at it, you knew it would not last long. Thus, the booty once captured on the *llanos* was to be returned to the *llanos* again, and our horse, thereby, became perhaps the first horse ever to have circumnavigated the Orinoco Delta.

While the party got going in earnest, and the mingling and rejoicing grew boisterous, another part of Serima buzzed with feverish but quiet activity. A revolution was taking place there, such as had not yet been seen in the tribe, and which was to fundamentally transform the balance of power in it. All the families who had felt threatened by the vengeful rule of the sorcerer Carapana and the evil chief Coneso gathered their belongings and slipped off to the settlement of the clan of the White Jaguar. No one dared to stop them: at that moment, everyone respected and feared our strength.

Soon, I got up and ordered my clan to leave the feast and return home. The day, now drawing to a close, had brought us a complete victory, and without shedding a single drop of blood, too, and an immeasurable joy overwhelmed us all. Now, back in our settlement, I went one by one to all my people and thanked each from the bottom of my heart, for they had all done an excellent job, but I reserved my heartiest hug to our four great sharpshooters, and I embraced those three who had fired the guns in the forest. And when we've had our fill of mutual congratulations, we proceeded with further, indispensable work: Arnak, in place of the still absent Manauri, assigned the newcomers to different huts, Vagura and his men set up sentries for the night, and I kept the rest of the men under arms for we dared not sleep peacefully as long as the Spaniards remained on the banks of the Imataca.

But nothing disturbed our peace that evening. The feast in Serima lasted well into the night, and eventually, the people slowly retired to sleep, the Arawaks in their huts and the Spaniards and the Chayma by their boats, tired, stuffed, and drunk. Slowly, gradually, all noises died down, yielding to the ordinary music of the jungle, the same as every night.

END OF EPISODE 3

TRANSLATOR'S SPECIAL REQUEST

Translating and publishing this book has been a labor of love for me.
I grew up reading it, and I have always wanted to be able
to share it with my American friends. And so here it is.
It will not make me rich, but if you liked the book, would you please
recommend it to a friend?
And give it an Amazon review?
https://www.amazon.com/dp/2919820494

THANK YOU!

Witold Makowiecki

Wind from the Hospitable Sea

Greece 562 BC. For insolvent debtors, the price of bankruptcy is slavery. When his
mother and siblings are seized for unpaid debts, little Diossos must run to fetch
help. He must cross mountains, forests, and stormy seas, brave wild animals, slave
catchers, pirates, and... the law. He has one month to achieve his quest but only
days to grow up.

Maria Rodziewiczówna

A Summer of the Forest Folk

The most beautiful book you will read this year.
Turn of the nineteenth century. Three women spend their summers in a remote
cottage deep in the last virgin forest in Europe. This summer, their teenage big-city
nephew joins them. A heart-warming, feel-good tale of love and friendship, of
coming of age, and of the healing power of nature. This is a book like nothing you
have ever read, a phenomenon, a genre of its own.

Jacek Bocheński
The Notorious Roman Trilogy

Divine Julius

"Would you like to become a god? It has been done before. There are
techniques." A great literary success at the time of its first appearance, the
book was almost immediately banned by the Communist regime. More
recently, it was banned by Facebook because "it might affect the way our
users vote."
*The Polish classic. Pure magnificence. This should not be read; it should
be savored. It is a filet mignon.*
ISBN: 978-9998793781

Naso the Poet

The loves and crimes of Rome's greatest poet. This beautifully and wittily
told story of Ovid was subjected to thousands of censorship edits, thereby
becoming possibly the world's most heavily censored book.
*It would be difficult to find a more brilliant fictional treatment of
Ovid's life than this hilariously serious entertainment.*
ISBN: 978-2919820047

Tiberius Caesar

The horrifying tale of Tiberius Caesar, the second emperor of Rome:
the man who normalized political terror. A moral, intellectual,
emotional zero whose only skill in life was to grab and hang onto
power. Be very afraid.
ISBN: 978-2919820047